Walter Savage Landor

Citation and examination of William Shakespeare

1595

Walter Savage Landor

Citation and examination of William Shakespeare
1595

ISBN/EAN: 9783337163846

Printed in Europe, USA, Canada, Australia, Japan

Cover: Foto ©Andreas Hilbeck / pixelio.de

More available books at **www.hansebooks.com**

CITATION AND EXAMINATION

OF

William Shakspeare

EUSEBY TREEN JOSEPH CARNABY AND

SILAS GOUGH Clerk

BEFORE THE WORSHIPFUL

SIR THOMAS LUCY Knight

TOUCHING DEER-STEALING

On the 19th day of September in the year of Grace 1582

NOW FIRST PUBLISHED FROM ORIGINAL PAPERS.

———◆———

TO WHICH IS ADDED

A Conference of Master Edmund Spenser

A GENTLEMAN OF NOTE

WITH

THE EARL OF ESSEX

TOUCHING THE STATE OF IRELAND A.D. 1595.

———

LONDON

SAUNDERS AND OTLEY CONDUIT STREET

M.DCCC.XXXIV.

EDITOR'S PREFACE.

" IT was an ancestor of my husband who *brought out* the famous Shakspeare."

These words were really spoken, and were repeated in conversation as most ridiculous. Certainly such was very far from the lady's intention; and who knows to what extent they are true ?

The frolic of Shakspeare in deer-stealing was the cause of his *Hegira ;* and his connexion with players in London

was the cause of his writing plays.   Had
he remained in his native town, his ambition had never been excited by the
applause of the intellectual, the popular,
and the powerful, which, after all, was
hardly sufficient to excite it.   He wrote
from the same motive as he acted; to
earn his daily bread.   He felt his own
powers, but he cared little for making
them felt by others more than served
his wants.

The malignant may doubt, or pretend
to doubt, the authenticity of the *Examination* here published.   Let us, who are
not malignant, be cautious of adding any
thing to the noisome mass of incredulity
that surrounds us : let us avoid the crying

sin of our age, in which the *Memoirs of a Parish Clerk,* edited as they were by a pious and learned dignitary of the established church, are questioned in regard to their genuineness; and even the privileges of Parliament are inadequate to cover from the foulest imputation, the imputation of having exercised his inventive faculties, the elegant and accomplished editor of Eugene Aram's apprehension, trial, and defence.

Indeed, there is little of real history, excepting in romances. Some of these are strictly true to nature; while histories in general give a distorted view of her, and rarely a faithful record either of momentous or of common events.

Examinations taken from the mouth are surely the most trust-worthy. Whoever doubts it may be convinced by Ephraim Barnett.

The Editor is confident he can give no offence to any person who may happen to bear the name of Lucy. The family of Sir Thomas became extinct nearly half a century ago, and the estates descended to the Rev. Mr. John Hammond, of Jesus College, in Oxford, a respectable Welsh curate, between whom and him there existed at his birth eighteen prior claimants. He took the name of Lucy.

The reader will form to himself, from this *Examination of Shakspeare,*

more favourable opinion of Sir Thomas
than is left upon his mind by the Dra-
matist in the character of Justice Shallow. The knight, indeed, is here ex-
hibited in all his pride of birth and
station, in all his pride of theologian
and poet; he is led by the nose, while
he believes that nobody can move him,
and shows some other weaknesses, which
the least attentive observer will discover;
but he is not without a little kindness at
the bottom of the heart — a heart too
contracted to hold much, or to let what
it holds ebulliate very freely. But, upon
the whole, we neither can utterly hate
nor utterly despise him. Ungainly as
he is,

Circum præcordia ludit.

The author of the *Imaginary Con-versations* seems, in his *Boccacio and Petrarca*, to have taken his idea of *Sir Magnus* from this manuscript. He, however, has adapted that character to the times; and in *Sir Magnus* the coward rises to the courageous, the unskilful in arms becomes the skilful, and war is to him a teacher of humanity. With much superstition, theology never molests him : scholarship and poetry are no affairs of his. He doubts of himself and others, and is as suspicious in his ignorance as Sir Thomas is confident.

With these wide diversities, there are family features, such as are likely to display themselves in different times and circumstances, and some so generically prevalent as never to lie quite dormant in the breed. In both of them there is parsimony, there is arrogance, there is contempt of inferiors, there is abject awe of power, there is irresolution, there is imbecility. But Sir Magnus has no knowledge, and no respect for it. Sir Thomas would almost go thirty miles, even to Oxford, to see a fine specimen of it, although, like most of those who call themselves the godly, he entertains the most undoubting belief that he is competent to correct the errors of the wisest and most practised theologian.

EXAMINATION,

ETC. ETC.

ABOUT one hour before noontide, the youth
William Shakspeare, accused of deer-stealing,
and apprehended for that offence, was brought
into the great hall at Charlecote, where, having
made his obeisance, it was most graciously permitted him to stand.

The worshipful Sir Thomas Lucy, Knight,
seeing him right opposite, on the farther side
of the long table, and fearing no disadvantage,
did frown upon him with great dignity; then,
deigning ne'er a word to the culprit, turned he
his face towards his chaplain, Sir Silas Gough,
who stood beside him, and said unto him most

courteously, and unlike unto one who in his own right commandeth,

"Stand out of the way! What are those two varlets bringing into the room?"

"The table, sir," replied Master Silas, "upon the which the consumption of the venison was perpetrated."

The youth, William Shakspeare, did thereupon pray and beseech his lordship most fervently, in this guise:

"O, sir! do not let him turn the tables against me, who am only a simple stripling, and he an old cogger."

But Master Silas did bite his nether lip, and did cry aloud,

"Look upon those deadly spots!"

And his worship did look thereupon most staidly, and did say in the ear of Master Silas, but in such wise that it reached even unto mine,

"Good honest chandlery, methinks!"

"God grant it may turn out so!" ejaculated Master Silas.

The youth, hearing these words, said unto him,

" I fear, Master Silas, gentry like you often pray God to grant what *he* would rather not; and now and then what *you* would rather not."

Sir Silas was wroth at this rudeness of speech about God in the face of a preacher, and said, reprovingly,

" Out upon thy foul mouth, knave! upon which lie slaughter and venison."

Whereupon did William Shakspeare sit mute awhile, and discomfited; then, turning toward Sir Thomas, and looking and speaking as one submiss and contrite, he thus appealed unto him :

" Worshipful sir! were there any signs of venison on my mouth, Master Silas could not for his life cry out upon it, nor help kissing it as 'twere a wench's."

Sir Thomas looked upon him with most lordly gravity and wisdom, and said unto him, in a voice that might have come from the bench,

"Youth! thou speakest irreverently;" and then unto Master Silas,—"Silas! to the business on hand. Taste the fat upon yon boor's table, which the constable hath brought hither, good Master Silas! And declare upon oath, being sworn in my presence, first, whether said fat do proceed of venison; secondly, whether said venison be of buck or doe."

Whereupon the reverend Sir Silas did go incontinently, and did bend forward his head, shoulders, and body, and did severally taste four white solid substances upon an oaken board; said board being about two yards long, and one yard four inches wide; found in, and brought thither from, the tenement or messuage of Andrew Haggit, who hath absconded. Of these four white solid substances, two were somewhat larger than a groat, and thicker; one about the size of King Henry the Eighth's shilling, when our late sovereign lord of blessed memory was towards the lustiest; and the other, that is to say the middlemost, did resemble in some sort a mushroom, not over fresh, turned upward on its stalk.

"And what sayest thou, Master Silas?" quoth the knight.

In reply whereunto Sir Silas thus averred:

"Venison! o' my conscience!
Buck! or burn me alive!

The three splashes in the circumference are verily and indeed venison; buck, moreover,— and Charlecote buck, upon my oath!"

Then carefully tasting the protuberance in the centre, he spat it out, crying,

"*Pho! pho! villain! villain!*" and shaking his fist at the culprit.

Whereat the said culprit smiled and winked, and said off-hand,

"Save thy spittle, Silas! It would supply a gaudy mess to the hungriest litter; but it would turn them from whelps into wolvets.

'Tis pity to throw the best of thee away. Nothing comes out of thy mouth that is not savoury and solid, bating thy wit, thy sermons, and thy promises."

It was my duty to write down the very words, irreverent as they are, being so commanded. More of the like, it is to be feared, would have ensued, but that Sir Thomas did check him, saying shrewdly,

" Young man! I perceive that if I do not stop thee in thy courses, thy name, being involved in thy company's, may one day or other reach across the county; and folks may handle it and turn it about, as it deserveth, from Coleshill to Nuneaton, from Bromwicham to Brownsover. And who knoweth but that, years after thy death, the very house wherein thou wert born may be pointed at, and commented on, by knots of people, gentle and simple! What a shame for an honest man's son! Thanks to me, who consider of measures to prevent it! Posterity shall laud and glorify me for plucking thee clean out of her head, and for picking up timely a ticklish skittle, that might overthrow with it a power of others just as light. I will rid the hundred of thee, with God's blessing!—nay, the whole shire. We will have none such in our county: we justices are agreed upon it, and we will keep our word now and for evermore. Wo betide any that resembles thee in any part of him!"

Whereunto Sir Silas added,

" We will dog him, and worry him, and haunt him, and bedevil him; and if ever he hear a comfortable word, it shall be in a language very different from his own."

" As different as thine is from a Christian's," said the youth.

" Boy! thou art slow of apprehension," said Sir Thomas, with much gravity; and, taking up the cue, did rejoin:

" Master Silas would impress upon thy ductile and tender mind the danger of evil doing; that we, in other words, that justice, is resolved to follow him up, even beyond his country, where he shall hear nothing better than the Italian or the Spanish, or the black language, or the language of Turk or Troubadour, or Tartar or Mongle. And, forsooth, for this gentle and indirect reproof, a gentleman in priest's orders is told by a stripling that he lacketh Christianity ! Who then shall give it ?"

WILLIAM SHAKSPEARE.

" Who, indeed? when the founder of the feast leaveth an invited guest so empty ! Yea, sir, the guest was invited, and the board was spread. The fruits that lay upon it be there still, and fresh as ever'; and the bread of life in those capacious canisters is unconsumed and unbroken."

SIR SILAS (*aside*).

" The knave maketh me hungry with his mischievous similitudes."

SIR THOMAS.

" Thou hast aggravated thy offence, Wil Shakspeare ! Irreverent caitiff ! is this a discourse for my chaplain and clerk? Can he or the worthy scribe Ephraim (his worship was pleased to call me worthy) write down such words as those, about litter and wolvets, for the perusal and meditation of the grand jury? If the whole corporation of Stratford had not unanimously given it against thee, still his tongue would catch thee, as the evet catcheth a gnat. Know, sirrah, the reverend Sir Silas, albeit ill appointed for riding, and not over-fond of it, goeth to every house wherein is a venison feast for thirty miles round. Not a buck's hoof on any stable-door but it awakeneth his recollections like a red letter."

This wholesome reproof did bring the youth back again to his right senses; and then said he, with contrition, and with a wisdom beyond his years, and little to be expected from one who had spoken just before so unavoidably and rashly,

" Well do I know it, your worship! And verily do I believe, that a bone of one being shovelled among the soil upon his coffin would forthwith quicken* him. Sooth to say, there is ne'er a buckhound in the county but he treateth him as a godchild, patting him on the head, soothing his velvety ear between thumb and fore-finger, ejecting tick from tenement, calling him *fine fellow, noble lad,* and giving him his blessing, as one dearer to him than a king's death to a debtor,† or a bastard to a dad of eighty. This is the only kindness I ever heard of Master Silas towards his fellow-creatures. Never hold me unjust, Sir Knight, to Master Silas. Could I learn other good of him, I would freely say it; for we do good by speaking it, and none is easier. Even bad men are not bad men while they praise the just. Their first step backward is more troublesome and wrenching to them than the first forward."

* Quicken, bring to life.

† Debtors were often let out of prison at the coronation of a new king, but creditors not paid by him.

" In God's name, where did he gather all this?" whispered his worship to the chaplain, by whose side I was sitting. " Why, he talks like a man of forty-seven, or more!"

" I doubt his sincerity, sir!" replied the chaplain. " His words are fairer now . . . .

, " Devil choke him for them!" interjected he with an undervoice.

" . . . . and almost book-worthy; but out of place. What the scurvy cur yelped against me, I forgive him as a Christian. Murrain upon such varlet vermin! It is but of late years that dignities have come to be reviled; the other parts of the Gospel were broken long before; this was left us; and now this likewise is to be kicked out of doors, amidst the mutterings of such mooncalves as him yonder."

" Too true, Silas!" said the knight, sighing deeply. " Things are not as they were in our glorious wars of York and Lancaster. The knaves were thinned then; two or three crops a-year of that rank bent grass which it has become the fashion of late to call the people. There was some difference then between buff doublets and iron mail; and the rogues felt it. Well-a-day! we must bear what God willeth, and never repine, although it gives a man the heart-ache. We are bound in duty to keep these things for the closet, and to tell God of them only when we call upon his holy name, and have him quite by ourselves."

Sir Silas looked discontented and impatient, and said snappishly,

" Cast we off here, or we shall be at fault. Start him, sir!—pr'ythee, start him."

Again his worship, Sir Thomas, did look gravely and grandly, and, taking a scrap of paper out of the Holy Book then lying before him, did read distinctly these words:

" Providence hath sent Master Silas back hither this morning to confound thee in thy guilt."

Again, with all the courage and composure

of an innocent man, and indeed with more than what an innocent man ought to possess in the presence of a magistrate, the youngster said, pointing toward Master Silas,

" The first moment he ventureth to lift up his visage from the table, hath Providence marked him miraculously. I have heard of black malice. How many of our words have more in them than we think of! Give a countryman a plough of silver, and he will plough with it all the season, and never know its substance. 'Tis thus with our daily speech. What riches lie hidden in the vulgar tongue of the poorest and most ignorant! What flowers of Paradise lie under our feet, with their beauties and parts undistinguished and undiscerned, from having been daily trodden on! O, sir, look you!—but let me cover my eyes! Look at his lips! Gracious Heaven! they were not thus when he entered: they are blacker now than Harry Tewe's bull-bitch's!"

Master Silas did lift up his eyes in astonishment and wrath; and his worship Sir Thomas did open his wider and wider, and cried by fits and starts,

" Gramercy! true enough! nay, afore God, too true by half!—I never saw the like!—Who would believe it!—I wish I were fairly rid of this examination!—my hands washed clean thereof!—Another time!—anon! We have our quarterly sessions! We are many together—at present, I remand . . . ."

And now, indeed, unless Sir Silas had taken his worship by the sleeve, he would mayhap have remanded the lad.   But Sir Silas still holding the sleeve, and shaking it, said hurriedly,

" Let me entreat your worship to ponder. What black does the fellow talk of? My blood and bile rose up against the rogue; but surely I did not turn black in the face, or in the mouth, as the fellow calls it?"

Whether Master Silas had some suspicion and inkling of the cause, or not, he rubbed his right hand along his face and lips, and, looking upon it, cried aloud,

" Ho! ho! is it off? There is some upon my finger's end, I find. Now I have it,—ay, there it is. That large splash upon the centre of the table is tallow, by my salvation! The profligates sat up until the candle burned out, and the last of it ran through the socket upon the board. We knew it before. I did convey into my mouth both fat and smut!"

" Many of your cloth and kidney do that, good Master Silas, and make no wry faces about it," quoth the youngster, with indiscreet merriment, although short of laughter, as became him, who had already stepped too far, and reached the mire.

To save paper and time, I shall now, for the most part, write only what they all said, not saying that they said it, and just copying out in my clearest hand what fell respectively from their mouths.

SIR SILAS.

" I did indeed spit it forth, and emunge my lips, as who should not?"

WILLIAM SHAKSPEARE.

" Would it were so!"

SIR SILAS.

" *Would it were so!* in thy teeth, hypocrite!"

SIR THOMAS.

" And, truly, I likewise do incline to hope and credit it, as thus paraphrased and expounded."

WILLIAM SHAKSPEARE.

" Wait until this blessed day next year, sir, at the same hour. You shall see it forth again at its due season: it would be no miracle if it lasted. Spittle may cure sore eyes, but not blasted mouths and scald consciences."

SIR THOMAS.

" Why! who taught thee all this?"

Then turned he leisurely toward Sir Silas, and placing his hand outspreaden upon the arm of the chaplain, said unto him in a low, judicial, hollow voice,

" Every word true and solemn! I have heard less wise saws from between black covers."

Sir Silas was indignant at this under-rating, as he appeared to think it, of the church and its ministry, and answered impatiently, with Christian freedom,

" Your worship surely will not listen to this wild wizard in his brothel-pulpit!"

WILLIAM SHAKSPEARE.

" Do I live to hear Charlecote Hall called a brothel-pulpit? Alas, then, I have lived too long!"

SIR SILAS.

" We will try to amend that for thee."

William seemed not to hear him, loudly as he spake and pointedly unto the youngster, who wiped his eyes, crying,

" Commit me, sir ! in mercy commit me ! Master Ephraim ! O, Master Ephraim ! A guiltless man may feel all the pangs of the guilty ! Is it you who are to make out the commitment ? Dispatch ! dispatch ! I am a-weary of my life. If I dared to lie, I would plead guilty."

SIR THOMAS.

" Heyday ! No wonder, Master Ephraim, thy entrails are moved and wamble. Dost weep, lad ? Nay, nay ; thou bearest up bravely. Silas, I now find, although the example come before me from humble life, that what my mother said was true —'twas upon my father's demise —' In great grief there are few tears.'"

Upon which did the youth, Willy Shakspeare, joy himself by the memory, and repeat these short verses, not wide from the same purport—

" There are, alas, some depths of woe
Too vast for tears to overflow."

SIR THOMAS.

" Let those who are sadly vexed in spirit mind that notion, whoever indited it, and be men. I always was; but some little griefs have pinched me woundily."

Master Silas grew impatient, for he had ridden hard that morning, and had no cushion upon his seat, as Sir Thomas had. I have seen in my time, that he who is seated on beech-wood hath very different thoughts and moralities from him who is seated on goose-feathers under doe-skin. But that is neither here nor there, albeit, an' I die, as I must, my heirs, Judith and her boy Elijah, may note it.

Master Silas, as above, looked sourishly, and cried aloud,

" The witnesses! the witnesses! testimony! testimony! We shall now see whose black goes deepest. There is a fork to be had that can hold the slipperiest eel, and a finger that can strip the slimiest. I cry your worship to the witnesses."

SIR THOMAS.

" Ay, indeed, we are losing the day: it wastes towards noon, and nothing done. Call the witnesses. How are they called by name? Give me the paper."

The paper being forthwith delivered into his worship's hand by the learned clerk, his worship did read aloud the name of Euseby Treen. Whereupon did Euseby Treen come forth through the great hall-door, which was ajar, and answer most audibly,

" Your worship !"

Straightway did Sir Thomas read aloud, in like form and manner, the name of Joseph Carnaby; and in like manner as aforesaid did Joseph Carnaby make answer and say,

" Your worship !"

Lastly did Sir Thomas turn the light of his countenance on William Shakspeare, saying,

" Thou seest these good men deponents against thee, William Shakspeare."

And then did Sir Thomas pause. And pending this pause did William Shakspeare look steadfastly in the faces of both; and, stroking down his own with the hollow of his hand from the jaw-bone to the chin-point, said unto his honour,

" Faith! it would give me much pleasure, and the neighbourhood much vantage, to see these two fellows good men. Joseph Carnaby and Euseby Treen! Why! your worship! they know every hare's form in Luddington-field better than their own beds, and as well pretty nigh as any wench's in the parish."

Then turned he, with jocular scoff, unto Joseph Carnaby, thus accosting him, whom his shirt, being made stiffer than usual for the occasion, rubbed and frayed.

" Ay, Joseph! smoothen and soothe thy

collar-piece again and again! Hark-ye! I know what smock that was knavishly cut from."

Master Silas rose up in high choler, and said unto Sir Thomas,

" Sir! do not listen to that lewd reviler: I wager ten groats I prove him to be wrong in his scent. Joseph Carnaby is righteous and discreet."

WILLIAM SHAKSPEARE.

" By daylight and before the parson. Bears and boars are tame creatures, and volubly discreet, in the sunshine and after dinner."

EUSEBY TREEN.

" I do know his down-goings and uprisings."

WILLIAM SHAKSPEARE.

" The man and his wife are one, saith holy Scripture."

EUSEBY TREEN.

" A sober-paced and rigid man, if such there be. Few keep Lent like unto him."

WILLIAM SHAKSPEARE.

" I warrant him, both lent and stolen."

SIR THOMAS.

" Peace and silence! Now, Joseph Carnaby, do thou depose on particulars."

JOSEPH CARNABY.

" May it please your worship! I was returning from Hampton upon Allhallowmass eve, between the hours of ten and eleven at night, in company with Master Euseby Treen; and when we came to the bottom of Mickle Meadow, we heard several men in discourse. I plucked Euseby Treen by the doublet, and whispered in his ear, ' Euseby! Euseby! let us slink along in the shadow of the elms and willows.'"

EUSEBY TREEN.

" *Willows and elm-trees* were the words."

WILLIAM SHAKSPEARE.

" See, your worship! what discordances! They cannot agree in their own story."

SIR SILAS.

" The same thing, the same thing, in the main."

WILLIAM SHAKSPEARE.

" By less differences than this estates have been lost, hearts broken, and England, our country, filled with homeless, helpless, destitute orphans.   I protest against it!"

SIR SILAS.

" Protest, indeed!   He talks as if he were a member of the House of Lords.   They alone can protest."

SIR THOMAS.

" Your attorney may *object*, not *protest*, before the lord judge.

" Proceed you, Joseph Carnaby."

JOSEPH CARNABY.

" In the shadow of the willows and elm-trees, then——

WILLIAM SHAKSPEARE.

" No hints, no conspiracies! Keep to your own story, man, and do not borrow his."

SIR SILAS.

" I over-rule the objection. Nothing can be more futile and frivolous."

WILLIAM SHAKSPEARE.

" So learned a magistrate as your worship will surely do me justice by hearing me attentively. I am young: nevertheless, having more than one year written in the office of an attorney, and having heard and listened to many discourses and questions on law, I cannot but remember the heavy fine inflicted on a gentleman of this county who committed a poor man to prison for being in possession of a hare, it being proved that the hare was in his possession, and not he in the hare's."

SIR SILAS.

" Synonymous term! synonymous term!"

SIR THOMAS.

" In what term sayest thou was it? I do not remember the case."

SIR SILAS.

" Mere quibble ! mere equivocation ! Jesuitical ! Jesuitical !"

WILLIAM SHAKSPEARE.

" It would be Jesuitical, Sir Silas, if it
dragged the law by its perversions to the side
of oppression and cruelty. The order of Jesuits,
I fear, is as numerous as its tenets are lax and
comprehensive. I am sorry to see their frocks
flounced with English serge."

SIR SILAS.

" I don't understand thee, viper!"

SIR THOMAS.

" Cease thou, Will Shakspeare! Know thy
place. And do thou, Joseph Carnaby, take up
again the thread of thy testimony."

JOSEPH CARNABY.

" We were still at some distance from the

party, when on a sudden Euseby hung an
. . . .*

SIR THOMAS.

" As well write *drew back*, Master Ephraim
and Master Silas! Be circumspecter in speech,
Master Joseph Carnaby! I did not look for
such rude phrases from that starch-warehouse
under thy chin.   Continue, man!''

JOSEPH CARNABY.

" ' Euseby,' said I in his ear, ' what ails
thee, Euseby?' ' I was no farther,' quoth he.
' What a number of names and voices!' "

SIR THOMAS.

" Dreadful gang! a number of names and
voices! Had it been any other day in the year
but Allhallowmas eve! To steal a buck upon

* The word here omitted is quite unintelligible. It
appears to have some reference to the language of the
Highlanders. That it was rough and outlandish, is appa-
rent from the reprimand of Sir Thomas.

such a day! Well! God may pardon even that. Go on, go on. But the laws of our country must have their satisfaction and atonement. Were it upon any other day in the calendar less holy, the buck were nothing, or next to nothing, saving the law and our conscience and our good report. Yet we, her majesty's justices, must stand in the gap, body and soul, against evil-doers. Now do thou, in furtherance of this business, give thine aid unto us, Joseph Carnaby! remembering that mine eye from this judgment-seat, and her majesty's bright and glorious one overlooking the whole realm, and the broader of God above, are upon thee."

Carnaby did quail a matter at these words about the judgment-seat and the broad eye, aptly and gravely delivered by him moreover who hath to administer truth and righteousness in our ancient and venerable laws, and especially at the present juncture in those against park-breaking and deer-stealing. But finally, nought discomfited, and putting his hand valiantly atwixt hip and midriff, so that his elbow well-nigh touched the taller pen in the ink-pot, he went on.

JOSEPH CARNABY.

" '*In the shadow of the willows and elm-trees,*' said he, '*and get nearer.*' We were still at some distance, maybe a score of furlongs, from the party——"

SIR THOMAS.

" Thou hast said it already—all save the score of furlongs.

" Hast room for them, Master Silas?"

" Yea," quoth Master Silas, " and would make room for fifty, to let the fellow swing at his ease."

SIR THOMAS.

" Hast room, Master Ephraim?"

" 'Tis done, most worshipful!" said I. The learned knight did not recollect that I could put fifty furlongs in a needle's eye, give me paper thin enough.

But far be it from me to vaunt of my penmanship, although there be those who do even in my own township and parish; yet they never have unperched me from my calling, and have had hard work to take an idle wench or two from under me on Saturday nights.

I do memorize thus much, not out of any malice or any soreness about me, but that those of my kindred into whose hands it please God these papers do fall hereafter, may bear up stoutly in such straits; and if they be good at the cudgel, that they, looking first at their man, do give it him heartily and unsparingly, keeping within law.

Sir Thomas, having overlooked what we had written, and meditated awhile thereupon, said unto Joseph,

" It appeareth by thy testimony that there was a huge and desperate gang of them a-foot. Revengeful dogs! it is difficult to deal with them. The laws forbid precipitancy and vio-lence. A dozen or two may return and harm

me; not me, indeed, but my tenants and servants. I would fain act with prudence, and
like unto him who looketh abroad. He must
tie his shoe tightly who passeth through mire;
he must step softly who steppeth over stones;
he must walk in the fear of the Lord (which,
without a brag, I do at this present feel upon
me,) who hopeth to reach the end of the
straightest road in safety."

SIR SILAS.

" Tut! tut! your worship! Her majesty's
deputy hath matchlocks and halters at a knight's
disposal, or the world were topsyturvy indeed."

SIR THOMAS.

" My mental ejaculations, and an influx of
grace thereupon, have shaken and washed from
my brain all thy last words, good Joseph! Thy
companion here, Euseby Treen, said unto thee
. . . ay . . ."

JOSEPH CARNABY.

" Said unto me, ' What a number of names
and voices! And there be but three living men

in all! And look again! Christ deliver us! all
the shadows save one go leftward: that one
lieth right upon the river. It seemeth a big
squat monster, shaking a little, as one ready to
spring upon its prey!"

SIR THOMAS.

" A dead man in his last agonies, no doubt!
Your deer-stealer doth boggle at nothing. He
hath alway the knife in doublet and the devil
at elbow.

" I wot not of any keeper killed or missing.
To lose one's deer and keeper too were over-
much.

" Do, in God's merciful name, hand unto
me a glass of sack, Master Silas! I wax faintish
at the big squat man. He hath harmed not
only me but mine. Furthermore, the examination is grown so long."

Then was the wine delivered by Sir Silas
into the hand of his worship, who drank it off
in a beaker of about half a pint, but little to
his satisfaction: for he said shortly afterwards,

" Hast thou poured no water into the sack, good Master Silas? It seemeth weaker and washier than ordinary, and affordeth small comfort unto the breast and stomach."

" Not I, truly, sir," replied Master Silas; " and the bottle is a fresh and sound one. The cork reported on drawing, as the best diver doth on sousing from Warwick bridge into Avon. A rare cork! as bright as the glass bottle, and as smooth as the lips of any cow."

SIR THOMAS.

" My mouth is out of taste this morning; or the same wine, mayhap, hath a different force and flavour in the dining-room and among friends. But to business—what more?"

" Joseph Carnaby, what may it be?" said I.

" I know," quoth he, " but dare not breathe it."

SIR THOMAS.

" I thought I had taken a glass of wine verily. Attention to my duty as a magistrate is paramount.   I mind nothing else when that lies before me.

" Carnaby ! I credit thy honesty, but doubt thy manhood.   Why not breathe it, with a vengeance ?"

JOSEPH CARNABY.

" It was Euseby who dared not."

SIR THOMAS.

" Stand still : say nothing yet : mind my orders : fair and softly : compose thyself."

They all stood silent for some time, and looked very composed, awaiting the commands of the knight.   His mind was clearly in such a state of devotion, that peradventure he might not have descended for a while longer to his mundane duties, had not Master Silas told him that, under the shadow of his wing, their courage had returned and they were quite composed again.

" You may proceed," said the knight.

JOSEPH CARNABY.

" Master Treen did take off his cap and

wipe his forehead.   I, for the sake of comforting him in this his heaviness, placed my hand upon his crown; and truly I might have taken it for a tuft of bents, the hair on end, the skin immovable as God's earth."

Sir Thomas, hearing these words, lifted up his hands above his own head, and, in the loudest voice he had yet uttered, did he cry,

" Wonderful are thy ways in Israel, O Lord !"

So saying, the pious knight did strike his knee with the palm of his right hand; and then gave he a sign, bowing his head and closing his eyes, by which Master Carnaby did think he signified his pleasure that he should go on deposing.   And he went on thus:

JOSEPH CARNABY.

" At this moment one of the accomplices cried, ' Willy! Willy! prythee stop! enough in all conscience!   First thou divertedst us from our undertaking with thy strange vagaries; thy

Italian girls' nursery sighs; thy Pucks and pinchings, and thy Windsor whimsies. No kitten upon a bed of marum ever played such antics. It was summer and winter, night and day with us within the hour; and with such religion did we think and feel it, we would have broken the man's jaw that gainsayed it. We have slept with thee under the oaks in the ancient forest of Arden, and we have wakened from our sleep in the tempest far at sea.* Now art thou for frightening us again out of all the senses thou hadst given us, with witches and women more murderous than they.'

" Then followed a deeper voice: ' Stouter men and more resolute are few; but thou, my lad, hast words too weighty for flesh and bones to bear up against. And who knows but these creatures may pop amongst us at last, as the wolf did, sure enough, upon him, the noisy

---

* By this deposition it would appear that Shakspeare had formed the idea, if not the outline, of several plays already, much as he altered them, no doubt, in after-life.

rogue, who so long had been crying *wolf!* and *wolf!*"

SIR THOMAS.

" Well spoken, for two thieves; albeit I miss the meaning of the most part. Did they prevail with the scapegrace and stop him?"

JOSEPH CARNABY.

" The last who had spoken did slap him on the shoulder, saying, ' Jump into the punt, lad, and across.' Thereupon did Will Shakspeare jump into said punt, and begin to sing a song about a mermaid."

WILLIAM SHAKSPEARE.

" Sir! is this credible? I will be sworn I never saw one; and verily do believe that scarcely one in a hundred years doth venture so far up the Avon."

SIR THOMAS.

" There is something in this. Thou mayest have sung about one, nevertheless. Young poets take great liberties with all female kind; not that mermaids are such very unlawful game for them, and there be songs even about worse and staler fish. Mind ye that! Thou hast written songs, and hast sung them, and lewd enough they be, God wot!"

WILLIAM SHAKSPEARE.

" Pardon me, your worship! they were not mine then. Peradventure the song about the mermaid may have been that ancient one which every boy in most parishes has been singing for many years, and, perhaps, his father before him; and somebody was singing it then, may-hap, to keep up his courage in the night."

SIR THOMAS.

" I never heard it."

WILLIAM SHAKSPEARE.

" Nobody would dare to sing in the pre-sence of your worship, unless commanded; not even the mermaid herself."

SIR THOMAS.

" Canst thou sing it?"

WILLIAM SHAKSPEARE.

" Verily, I can sing nothing."

SIR THOMAS.

" Canst thou repeat it from memory ?"

WILLIAM SHAKSPEARE.

" It is so long since I have thought about it, that I may fail in the attempt."

SIR THOMAS.

" Try, however."

WILLIAM SHAKSPEARE.

" The mermaid sat upon the rocks
   All day long,
  Admiring her beauty and combing her locks,
   And singing a mermaid song."

SIR THOMAS.

" What was it? what was it? I thought as much. There thou standest, like a woodpecker, chattering and chattering, breaking the bark with thy beak, and leaving the grub where it was. This is enough to put a saint out of patience."

WILLIAM SHAKSPEARE.

" The wishes of your worship possess a mysterious influence : I now remember all.

" And hear the mermaid's song you may,
    As sure as sure can be,
If you will but follow the sun all day,
    And souse with him into the sea."

SIR THOMAS.

" It must be an idle fellow who would take that trouble: besides, unless he nicked the time he might miss the monster. There be many who are slow to believe that the mermaid singeth."

WILLIAM SHAKSPEARE.

" Ah, sir! not only the mermaid singeth, but the merman sweareth, as another old song will convince you.

SIR THOMAS.

" I would fain be convinced of God's wonders in the great deeps, and would lean upon the weakest reed like unto thee to manifest his glory. Thou mayest convince me."

WILLIAM SHAKSPEARE.

1.

" A wonderful story, my lasses and lads,
    Peradventure you've heard from your grannams or dads,

Of a merman that came every night to woo
The spinster of spinsters, our Catherine Crewe.

2.

But Catherine Crewe
Is now seventy-two,
And avers she hath half forgotten
The truth of the tale, when you ask her about it,
And says, as if fain to deny it or flout it,
Poo! the merman is dead and rotten.

3.

The merman came up, as the mermen are wont,
To the top of the water, and then swam upon't;
And Catherine saw him with both her two eyes,
A lusty young merman full six feet in size.

4.

And Catherine was frighten'd,
Her scalp-skin it tighten'd,
And her head it swam strangely, although on dry land;
And the merman made bold
Eftsoons to lay hold
(*This* Catherine well recollects) of her hand.

5.

But how could a merman, if ever so good,
Or if ever so clever, be well understood
By a simple young creature of our flesh and blood?

6.

Some tell us the merman
Can only speak German,
In a voice between grunting and snoring;
But Catherine says he had learnt in the wars
The language, persuasions, and oaths of our tars,
And that even his voice was not foreign.

7.

Yet when she was asked how he managed to hide
The green fishy tail, coming out of the tide
For night after night above twenty,
' You troublesome creatures!' old Catherine replied,
' *In his pocket :* won't that now content ye?'"

SIR THOMAS.

" I have my doubts yet.　I should have said unto her seriously, ' Kate! Kate! I am not convinced.'　There may be witchcraft or sortilege in it.　I would have made it a star-chamber matter."

WILLIAM SHAKSPEARE.

" It was one, sir!"

SIR THOMAS.

" And now I am reminded by this silly

childish song, which, after all, is not the true mermaid's, thou didst tell me, Silas, that the papers found in the lad's pocket were intended for poetry."

SIR SILAS.

" I wish he had missed his aim, sir, in your park, as he hath missed it in his poetry. The papers are not worth reading ; they do not go against him in the point at issue."

SIR THOMAS.

" We must see that ; they being taken upon his person when apprehended."

SIR SILAS.

" Let Ephraim read them then : it behoveth not me, a Master of Arts, to con a whelp's whining."

SIR THOMAS.

" Do thou read them aloud unto us, good Master Ephraim."

Whereupon I took the papers which young Willy had not bestowed much pains on ; and

they posed and puzzled me grievously, for they
were blotted and scrawled in many places, as
if somebody had put him out. These likewise
I thought fit, after long consideration, to write
better, and preserve, great as the loss of time
is when men of business take in hand such
unseemly matters. However, they are decenter
than most, and not without their moral: for
example :—

" TO THE OWLET.

Who, O thou sapient saintly bird!
Thy shouted warnings ever heard
      Unbleached by fear?
The blue-faced blubbering imp, who steals
Yon turnips, thinks thee at his heels,
      Afar or near.

The brawnier churl, who brags at times
To front and top the rankest crimes—
      To paunch a deer,
Quarter a priest, or squeeze a wench,
Scuds from thee, clammy as a tench,
      He knows not where.

For this the righteous Lord of all
Consigns to thee the castle-wall,

When, many a year,
Closed in the chancel-vault, are eyes
Rainy or sunny at the sighs
Of knight or peer."

Sir Thomas, when I had ended, said unto me,

" No harm herein ; but are they over ?"

I replied, " Yea, sir !"

" I miss the *posy*," quoth he; " there is usually a lump of sugar, or a smack thereof, at the bottom of the glass. They who are inexperienced in poetry do write it as boys do their copies in the copy-book, without a flourish at the finis. It is only the master who can do this befittingly."

I bowed unto his worship reverentially, thinking of a surety he meant me, and returned my best thanks in set language. But his worship rebuffed them, and told me graciously that he had an eye on another of very different quality ; that the plain sense of his discourse might do for me, the subtiler was certainly for himself. He added, that in his younger days he had heard from a person of great parts, and had since profited by it, that ordinary poets are like adders—the tail blunt and the body rough, and the whole reptile cold-blooded and sluggish; whereas we, he subjoined, leap and caracole and curvet, and are as warm as velvet, and as sleek as satin, and as perfumed as a Naples fan, in every part of us; and the end of our poems is as pointed as a perch's back-fin, and it requires as much nicety to pick it up as a needle* at nine groats the hundred."

Then turning towards the culprit, he said mildly unto him,

" Now why canst thou not apply thyself

---

* The greater part of the value of the present work arises from the certain information it affords us on the price of small needles in the reign of Elizabeth: fine needles in her days were made only at Liege, and some few cities in the Netherlands, and may be reckoned among those things which were much dearer than they are now.

unto study? Why canst thou not ask advice of thy superiors in rank and wisdom? In a few years, under good discipline, thou mightest rise from the owlet unto the peacock. I know not what pleasant things might not come into the youthful head thereupon.

"He was the bird of Venus,* goddess of beauty. He flew down (I speak as a poet, and not in my quality of knight and Christian) with half the stars of heaven upon his tail; and his long blue neck doth verily appear a dainty slice out of the solid sky."

Sir Silas smote me with his elbow, and said in my ear,

"He wanteth not this stuffing: he beats a pheasant out of the kitchen, to my mind, take him only at the pheasant's size, and don't (upon your life) overdo him."

"Never be cast down in spirit, nor take it too grievously to heart, if the colour be a suspicion of the pinkish — no sign of rawness in

---

* Mr. Took had not yet published his *Pantheon*.

that : none whatever.   It is as becoming to him as to the salmon ; it is as natural to your pea-chick in his best cookery, as it is to the finest October morning — moist underfoot, when par-tridge's and puss's and renard's scent lies sweetly."

Willy Shakspeare in the meantime lifted up his hands above his ears half a cubit, and, taking breath again, said audibly, although he willed it to be said unto himself alone,

" O that knights could deign to be our teachers !   Methinks I should briefly spring up into heaven, through the very chink out of which the peacock took his neck."

Master Silas, who, like myself and the worshipful knight, did overhear him, said angrily,

" To spring up into heaven, my lad, it would be as well to have at least one foot upon the ground to make the spring withal. I doubt whether we shall leave thee this vantage."

" Nay, nay! thou art hard upon him, Silas!" said the knight.

I was turning over the other papers taken from the pocket of the culprit on his apprehension, and had fixed my eyes on one, when Sir Thomas caught them thus occupied, and exclaimed,

" Mercy upon us! have we more ?"

" Your patience, worshipful sir!" said I ; " must I forward ?"

" Yea, yea," quoth he, resignedly, " we must go through : we are pilgrims in this life."

Then did I read, in a clear voice, the contents of paper the second, being as followeth :

"THE MAID'S LAMENT.

" I loved him not; and yet, now he is gone,
    I feel I am alone.
I check'd him while he spoke; yet, could he speak,
    Alas ! I would not check.
For reasons not to love him once I sought,
    And wearied all my thought
To vex myself and him: I now would give
    My love could he but live

D

Who lately lived for me, and, when he found
    'Twas vain, in holy ground
He hid his face amid the shades of death!
    I waste for him my breath
Who wasted his for me! but mine returns,
    And this lorn bosom burns
With stifling heat, heaving it up in sleep,
    And waking me to weep
Tears that had melted his soft heart: for years
    Wept he as bitter tears!
Merciful God! such was his latest prayer,
    These may she never share!
Quieter is his breath, his breast more cold,
    Than daisies in the mould,
Where children spell, athwart the churchyard gate,
    His name and life's brief date.
Pray for him, gentle souls, whoe'er you be,
    And, oh! pray too for me!"

Sir Thomas had fallen into a most comfortable and refreshing slumber ere this lecture was concluded: but the pause broke it, as there be many who experience after the evening service in our parish-church. Howbeit, he had presently all his wits about him, and remembered well that he had been carefully counting the syllables, about the time when I had pierced as far as into the middle.

" Young man," said he to Willy, " thou givest short measure in every other sack of the load. Thy uppermost stake is of right length; the undermost falleth off, methinks.

" Master Ephraim, canst thou count syllables? I mean no offence. I may have counted wrongfully myself, not being born nor educated for an accountant."

At such order I did count; and truly the suspicion was as just as if he had neither been a knight nor a sleeper.

" Sad stuff! sad stuff, indeed!" said Master Silas, " and smelling of popery and wax-candles."

" Ay?" said Sir Thomas, " I must sift that."

" If praying for the dead is not popery," said Master Silas, " I know not what the devil is. Let them pray for us; they may know whether it will do us any good: we need not pray for them ; we cannot tell whether it will do them any. I call this sound divinity."

" Are our churchmen all `agreed thereupon ?" asked Sir Thomas.

"The wisest are," replied Master Silas. " There are some lank rascals who will never agree upon any thing but upon doubting. I would not give ninepence for the best gown upon the most thrifty of 'em ; and their fingers are as stiff and hard with their pedlary knavish writing, as any bishop's are with chalk-stones won honestly from the gout."

Sir Thomas took the paper up from the table on which I had laid it, and said, after a while,

" The man may only have swooned. I scorn to play the critic, or to ask any one the meaning of a word ; but, sirrah !"

Here he turned in his chair from the side of Master Silas, and said unto Willy,

" William Shakspeare ! out of this thraldom in regard to popery, I hope, by God's blessing, to deliver thee.   If ever thou repeatest the said verses, knowing the man to be to all intents and purposes a dead man, prythee read the censurable line as thus corrected,

' Pray for our Virgin Queen, gentles ! whoe'er you be,'

although it is not quite the thing that another should impinge so closely on her skirts.

" By this improvement, of me suggested, thou mayest make some amends—a syllable or two —for the many that are weighed in the balance and are found wanting."

Then turning unto me, as being conversant by my profession in such matters, and the same being not very worthy of learned and staid clerks the like of Master Silas, he said,

" Of all the youths that did ever write in verse, this one verily is he who hath the fewest flowers and devices.   But it would be loss of time to form a border, in the fashion of a kingly crown, or a dragon, or a Turk on horseback, out of buttercups and dandelions.

" Master Ephraim ! look at these badgers ! with a long leg on one quarter and a short leg on the other. The wench herself might well and truly have said all that matter without the poet, bating the rhymes and metre. Among the girls in the country there are many such *shilly-shallys*, who give themselves sore eyes and sharp eye-water : I would cure them rod in hand."

Whereupon did William Shakspeare say, with great humility,

" So would I, may it please your worship, an they would let me."

" Incorrigible sluts ! Out upon 'em ! and thou art no better than they are," quoth the knight.

Master Silas cried aloud, " No better, marry ! they at the worst are but carted and whipt for the edification of the market-folks.* Not a squire or parson in the county round but comes in his best to see a man hanged."

* This was really the case within our memory.

" The edification then is higher by a deal," said William, very composedly.

" Troth ! is it," replied Master Silas. "The most poisonous reptile has the richest jewel in his head : thou shalt share the richest gift bestowed upon royalty, and shalt cure the king's evil."*

" It is more tractable, then, than the church's," quoth William ; and, turning his face towards the chair, he made an obeisance to Sir Thomas, saying,

" Sir ! the more submissive my behaviour is, the more vehement and boisterous is Master Silas. My gentlest words serve only to carry him towards the contrary quarter, as the south wind bloweth a ship northward."

" Youth !" said Sir Thomas, smiling most

* It was formerly thought, and perhaps is thought still, that the hand of a man recently hanged being rubbed on the tumour of the king's evil was able to cure it. The crown and the gallows divided the glory of the sovereign remedy.

benignly, " I find, and well indeed might I have surmised, thy utter ignorance of winds, equinoxes, and tides.   Consider now a little! With what propriety can a wind be called the south wind if it bloweth a vessel to the north? Would it be a south wind that blew it from this hall into Warwick market-place?"

" It would be a strong one," said Master Silas unto me, pointing his remark, as witty men are wont, with the elbow-pan.

But Sir Thomas, who waited for an answer, and received none, continued,

" Would a man be called a good man who tended and pushed on towards evil?"

WILLIAM SHAKSPEARE.

" I stand corrected.   I could sail to Cathay or Tartary* with half the nautical knowledge I have acquired in this glorious hall.

" The devil impelling a mortal to wrong courses, is thereby known to be the devil.   He,

* And yet he never did sail any farther than into Bohemia.

on the contrary, who exciteth to good is no
devil, but an angel of light, or under the guid-
ance of one. The devil driveth unto his own
home ; so doth the south wind, so doth the
north wind.

" Alas! alas! we possess not the mastery
over our own weak minds, when a higher spirit
standeth nigh, and draweth us within his influence."

SIR THOMAS.

" Those thy words are well enough — very
well, very good, wise, discreet, judicious beyond
thy years. But then that *sailing* comes in an
awkward, ugly way across me — that *Cathay,*
that *Tartarus!*

" Have a care! Do thou nothing rashly.
Mind! an thou stealest my punt for the purpose, I send the constable after thee or e'er thou
art half way over."

WILLIAM SHAKSPEARE.

" He would make a stock-fish of me an he
caught me. It is hard sailing out of his straits,

although they be carefully laid down in most
parishes, and many have taken them from
actual survey."

SIR SILAS.

" Sir, we have bestowed on him already
well-nigh a good hour of our time."

Sir Thomas, who was always fond of giving
admonition and reproof to the ignorant and
erring, and who had found the seeds (little
mustard-seeds, 'tis true, and never likely to
arise into the great mustard-tree of the Gospel)
in the poor lad Willy, did let his heart soften a
whit tenderer and kindlier than Master Silas
did, and said unto Master Silas,

" A good hour of our time! Yea, Silas!
and thou wouldst give *him* eternity !"

" What, sir ! would you let him go ?" said
Master Silas. " Presently we shall have neither deer nor dog, neither hare nor coney,
neither swan nor heron ; every carp from pool,
every bream from brook, will be groped for.
The marble monuments in the church will no

longer protect the leaden coffins; and if there be any ring of gold on the finger of knight or dame, it will be torn away with as little ruth and ceremony as the ring from a butchered sow's snout."

" Awful words! Master Silas," quoth the knight, musing; " but thou mistakest my intentions.   I let him not go: howbeit, at worst I would only mark him in the ear, and turn him up again after this warning, peradventure with a few stripes to boot athwart the shoulders, in order to make them shrug a little, and shake off the burden of idleness."

Now I, having seen, I dare not say the innocence, but the innocent and simple manner of Willy, and pitying his tender years, and having an inkling that he was a lad, poor Willy! whom God had endowed with some parts, and into whose breast he had instilled that milk of loving-kindness by which alone we can be like unto those little children of whom is the household and kingdom of our Lord, I was moved, yea even unto tears. And now, to bring gentler thoughts into the hearts of Master Silas and Sir Thomas, who, in his wisdom, deemed it a light punishment to slit an ear or two, or inflict a wiry scourging, I did remind his worship that another paper was yet unread, at least to them, although I had been perusing it.

This was much pleasanter than the two former, and overflowing with the praises of the worthy knight and his gracious lady; and having an echo to it in another voice, I did hope thereby to disarm their just wrath and indignation. It was thus couched:—

" FIRST SHEPHERD.

" Jesu! what lofty elms are here!
Let me look through them at the clear
Deep sky above, and bless my star
That such a worthy knight's they are!

" SECOND SHEPHERD.

" Innocent creatures! how the deer
Tròt merrily, and romp and rear!

" FIRST SHEPHERD.

" The glorious knight who walks beside
His most majestic lady bride,

" SECOND SHEPHERD.

" Under these branches spreading wide,

" FIRST SHEPHERD.

" Carries about so many cares
  Touching his ancestors and heirs,
  That came from Athens and from Rome —

" SECOND SHEPHERD.

" As many of them as are come —

" FIRST SHEPHERD.

" Nought else the smallest lodge can find
  In the vast manors of his mind;
  Envying not Solomon his wit —

" SECOND SHEPHERD.

" No, nor his women not a bit;
  Being well-built and well-behaved
  As Solomon, I trow, or David.

" FIRST SHEPHERD.

" And taking by his jewell'd hand
  The jewel of that lady bland,
  He sees the tossing antlers pass
  And throw quaint shadows o'er the grass;
  While she alike the hour beguiles,
  And looks at him and them, and smiles.

" SECOND SHEPHERD.

" With conscience proof 'gainst Satan's shock,
 Albeit finer than her smock,*
 Marry ! her smiles are not of vanity,
 But resting on sound Christianity.
 Faith you would swear had nail'd† her ears on
 The book and cushion of the parson."

" Methinks the rhyme at the latter end might be bettered," said Sir Thomas. " The remainder is indited not unaptly. But, young man ! never having obtained the permission of my honourable dame to praise her in guise of poetry, I cannot see all the merit I would fain discern in the verses. She ought first to have been sounded; and it being certified that she disapproved not her glorification, then might it be trumpeted forth into the world below."

* *Smock*, formerly a part of the female dress, corresponding with *shroud*, or what we now call (or lately called) *shirt* of the man's. Fox, speaking of Latimer's death, says, " Being slipped into his *shroud*."

† Faith nailing the ears is a strong and sacred metaphor. The rhyme is imperfect: Shakspeare was not always attentive to these minor beauties.

" Most worshipful knight!" replied the youngster; " I never could take it in hand to sound a dame of quality: they are all of them too deep and too practised for me, and have better and abler men about 'em. And surely I did imagine to myself, that if it were asked of any honourable man (omitting to speak of ladies) whether he would give permission to be openly praised, he would reject the application as a gross offence. It appeareth to me that even to praise one's-self, although it be shameful, is less shameful than to throw a burning coal into the incense-box that another doth hold to waft before us, and then to snift and simper over it, with maidenly wishful coyness, as if forsooth one had no hand in setting it asmoke."

Then did Sir Thomas, in his zeal to instruct the ignorant, and so make the lowly hold up their heads, say unto him,

" Nay, but all the great do thus. Thou must not praise them without leave and license. Praise unpermitted is plebeian praise. It is presumption to suppose that thou knowest enough of the noble and the great to discover their high qualities. They alone could manifest them unto thee. It requireth much discernment and much time to enucleate and bring into light their abstruse wisdom and gravely featured virtues. Those of ordinary men lie before thee in thy daily walks: thou mayest know them by converse at their tables, as thou knowest the little tame squirrel that chippeth his nuts in the open sunshine of a bowling-green. But beware how thou enterest the awful arbours of the great, who conceal their magnanimity in the depths of their hearts, as lions do."

He then paused; and observing the youth in deep and earnest meditation over the fruits of his experience, as one who tasted and who would fain digest them, he gave him encouragement, and relieved the weight of his musings by kind interrogation:

" So, then, these verses are thine own?"

The youth answered,

" Sir, I must confess my fault."

SIR THOMAS.

" And who was the shepherd written here *Second Shepherd,* that had the ill manners to interrupt thee ? Methinks, in helping thee to mount the saddle, he pretty nigh tossed thee over,* with his jerks and quirks."

Without waiting for any answer, his worship continued his interrogations :

---

* Shakspeare seems to have profited afterwards by this metaphor, even more perhaps than by all the direct pieces of instruction in poetry given him so handsomely by the worthy knight. And here it may be permitted the Editor to profit also by the manuscript, correcting in Shakspeare what is absolute nonsense as now printed :

Vaulting ambition that o'erleaps *itself.*

It should be its *sell.* *Sell* is *saddle* in Spenser and else-where, from the Latin and Italian.

This emendation was shewn to the late Mr. Hazlitt, an acute man at least, who expressed his conviction that it was the right reading, and added somewhat more in approbation of it.

" But do you woolstaplers call yourselves by the style and title of shepherds?"

WILLIAM SHAKSPEARE.

" Verily, sir, do we; and I trust by right. The last owner of any place is called the master more properly than the dead and gone who once held it. If that be true (and who doubts it?) we, who have the last of the sheep, namely the wool and skin, and who buy all of all the flock, surely may more properly be called shepherds, than those idle vagrants who tend them only for a season, selling a score or purchasing a score, as may happen."

Here Sir Thomas did pause awhile, and then said unto Master Silas,

" My own cogitations, and not this stripling, have induced me to consider and to conclude a weighty matter for knightly scholarship. I never could rightly understand before how Colin Clout, and sundry others calling themselves shepherds, should argue like doctors in law, physic, and divinity.

" Silas! they were woolstaplers; and they must have exercised their wits in dealing with tithe-proctors and parsons, and moreover with fellows of colleges from our two learned universities, who have sundry lands held under them, as thou knowest, and take the small tithes in kind. Colin Clout, methinks, from his extensive learning, might have acquired enough interest with the Queen's Highness to change his name for the better, and, furthermore, her royal license to carry armorial bearings, in no peril of taint from so unsavoury an appellation."

Master Silas did interrupt this discourse, by saying,

" May it please your worship, the constable is waiting."

Whereat Sir Thomas said tartly,

" And let him wait."*

Then to me,

---

* It has been suggested that this answer was borrowed from Virgil, and goes strongly against the genuineness of the manuscript. The Editor's memory was upon the

" I hope we have done with verses, and are not to be befooled by the lad's nonsense touching mermaids or worse creatures."

Then to Will,

" William Shakspeare! we live in a Christian land, a land of great toleration and forbearance. Threescore cartsful of faggots a-year are fully sufficient to clear our English air from every pestilence of heresy and witchcraft. It hath not alway been so, God wot! Innocent and guilty took their turns before the fire, like geese and capons. The spit was never cold; the cook's sleeve was ever above the elbow. Countrymen came down from distant villages, into towns and cities, to see perverters whom they had never heard of, and to learn the righteousness of hatred. When heretics waxed

stretch to recollect the words: the learned critic supplied them :

" Solum Æneas vocat : *et vocet*, oro."

The Editor could only reply, indeed weakly, that *calling* and *waiting* are not exactly the same, unless when tradesmen rap and gentlemen are leaving town.

fewer, the religious began to grumble, that God, in losing his enemies, had also lost his avengers.

" Do not thou, William Shakspeare, dig the hole for thy own stake. If thou canst not make men wise, do not make them merry at thy cost. We are not to be paganised any more. Having struck from our calendars, and unnailed from our chapels, many dozens of decent saints, with as little compunction and remorse as unlucky lads throw frog-spawn and tadpoles out of stagnant ditches, never let us think of bringing back amongst us the daintier divinities they ousted. All these are the devil's imps, beautiful as they appear in what we falsely call works of genius, which really and truly are the devil's own—statues more graceful than humanity, pictures more living than life, eloquence that raised single cities above empires, poor men above kings. If these are not Satan's works, where are they? I will tell thee where they are likewise. In holding vain converse with false gods. The utmost we can allow in propriety is to call a knight Phœbus, and a dame Diana. They are not meat for every trencher.

"We must now proceed straightforward with the business on which thou comest before us. What further sayest thou, witness?

EUSEBY TREEN.

"His face was toward me: I saw it clearly. The graver man followed him into the punt, and said, roughly, 'We shall get hanged as sure as thou pipest.'

"Whereunto he answered,

> 'Naturally, as fall upon the ground
> The leaves in winter and the girls in spring.'

And then began he again with the mermaid: whereat the graver man clapped a hand before his mouth, and swore he should take her in wedlock, to have and to hold, if he sang another stave. 'And thou shalt be her pretty little bridemaid,' quoth he gaily to the graver man, chucking him under the chin."

SIR THOMAS.

" And what did Carnaby say unto thee, or what didst thou say unto Carnaby?"

EUSEBY TREEN.

" Carnaby said unto me, somewhat tauntingly, ' The big squat man, that lay upon thy bread-basket like a nightmare, is a punt at last, it seems.'

"' Punt, and more too,' answered I. ' Tarry awhile, and thou shalt see this punt (so let me call it) lead them into temptation, and swamp them, or carry them to the gallows: I would not stay else."

SIR THOMAS.

" And what didst thou, Joseph Carnaby?

JOSEPH CARNABY.

" Finding him neither slack nor shy, I readily tarried. We knelt down opposite each other, and said our prayers; and he told me he was now comfortable. ' The evil one,' said he, ' hath enough to mind yonder: he shall not hurt us.'

" Never was a sweeter night, had there been but some mild ale under it, which any one would have sworn it was made for. The milky way looked like a long drift of hail-stones on a sunny ridge."

SIR THOMAS.

" Hast thou done describing?"

JOSEPH CARNABY.

" Yea, an please your worship."

SIR THOMAS.

" God's blessing be upon thee, honest Carnaby! I feared a moon-fall. In our days nobody can think about a plum-pudding but the moon comes down upon it. I warrant ye this lad here hath as many moons in his poems as the Saracens had in their banners."

WILLIAM SHAKSPEARE.

" I have not hatched mine yet, sir. Whenever I do I trust it will be worth taking to market."

JOSEPH CARNABY.

" I said all I know of the stars; but Master

Euseby can run over half a score and upwards, here and there. 'Am I right or wrong?' cried he, spreading on the back of my hand all his fingers, stiff as antlers and cold as icicles. ' Look up, Joseph! Joseph! there is no Lucifer in the firmament.' I myself did feel queerish and qualmy upon hearing that a star was missing, being no master of gainsaying it; and I abased my eyes, and entreated of Euseby to do in like manner. And in this posture did we both of us remain; and the missing star did not disquiet me; and all the others seemed as if they knew us and would not tell of us; and there was peace and pleasantness over sky and earth. And I said to my companion,

" ' How quiet now, good Master Euseby, are all God's creatures in this meadow, because they never pry into such high matters, but breathe sweetly among the pig-nuts. The only things we hear or see stirring are the glow-worms and dormice, as though they were sent for our edification, teaching us to rest con-

tented with our own little light, and to come
out and seek our sustenance where none molest
or thwart us.'"

WILLIAM SHAKSPEARE.

" Ye would have it thus, no doubt, when
your pockets and pouches are full of gins and
nooses."

SIR THOMAS.

" A bridle upon thy dragon's tongue! And
do thou, Master Joseph, quit the dormice and
glow-worms, and tell us whither did the
rogues go."

JOSEPH CARNABY.

" I wot not after they had crossed the river:
they were soon out of sight and hearing."

SIR THOMAS.

" Went they towards Charlecote?"

JOSEPH CARNABY.

" Their first steps were thitherward."

SIR THOMAS.

" Did they come back unto the punt?"

JOSEPH CARNABY.

" They went down the stream in it, and crossed the Avon some fourscore yards below where we were standing. They came back in it, and moored it to the sedges in which it had stood before."

SIR THOMAS.

" How long were they absent ?"

JOSEPH CARNABY.

" Within an hour, or thereabout, all the three men returned. Will Shakspeare and another were sitting in the middle, the third punted.

" ' Remember now, gentles ! ' quoth William Shakspeare, ' the road we have taken is henceforward a footpath for ever, according to law.'

" ' How so ?' asked the punter, turning towards him.

" ' Forasmuch as a corpse hath passed along it,' answered he.

" Whereupon both Euseby and myself did

forthwith fall upon our faces, commending our souls unto the Lord."

SIR THOMAS.

" It was then really the dead body that quivered so fearfully upon the water, covering all the punt! Christ, deliver us! I hope the keeper they murdered was not Jeremiah. His wife and four children would be very chargeable, and the man was by no means amiss. Proceed! what further?"

" On reaching the bank, ' I never sat pleasanter in my lifetime,' said William Shakspeare, ' than upon this carcass.'"

SIR THOMAS.

" Lord have mercy upon us! Thou upon a carcass, at thy years!"

And the knight drew back his chair half an ell further from the table, and his lips quivered at the thought of such inhumanity.

" And what said he more? and what did he?" asked the knight.

JOSEPH CARNABY.

" He patted it smartly, aud said, ' Lug it out ; break it.' "

SIR THOMAS.

" These four poor children ! who shall feed them ? "

SIR SILAS.

" Sir ! in God's name have you forgotten that Jeremiah is gone to Nun-Eaton to see his father, and that the murdered man is the buck ? "

SIR THOMAS.

" They killed the buck likewise. But what, ye cowardly varlets ! have ye been deceiving me all this time ? And thou, youngster ! couldst thou say nothing to clear up the case ? Thou shalt smart for it. Methought I had lost by a violent death the best servant ever man had—righteous, if there be no blame in saying it, as the prophet whose name he beareth, and brave as the lion of Judah."

WILLIAM SHAKSPEARE.

" Sir, if these men could deceive your worship for a moment, they might deceive me for ever. I could not guess what their story aimed at, except my ruin. I am inclined to lean for once towards the opinion of Master Silas, and to believe it was really the stolen buck on which this William (if indeed there is any truth at all in the story) was sitting."

SIR THOMAS.

" What more hast thou for me that is not enigma or parable?"

JOSEPH CARNABY.

" I did not see the carcass, man's or beast's, may it please your worship, and I have re-cited and can recite that only which I saw and heard. After the words of lugging out and breaking it, knives were drawn accordingly. It was no time to loiter or linger. We crope back under the shadow of the alders and hazels on the high bank that bordereth Micklen

Meadow, and, making straight for the public road, hastened homeward."

SIR THOMAS.

" Hearing this deposition, dost thou affirm the like upon thy oath, Master Euseby Treen, or dost thou vary in aught essential?"

EUSEBY TREEN.

" Upon my oath I do depose and affirm the like, and truly the identical same; and I will never more vary upon aught essential."

SIR THOMAS.

" I do now further demand of thee whether thou knowest any thing more appertaining unto this business."

EUSEBY TREEN.

" Ay, verily : that your worship may never hold me for timorsome and superstitious, I do furthermore add that some other than deer-stealers was abroad. In sign whereof, although it was the dryest and clearest night of the season, my jerkin was damp inside and outside when I reached my house-door."

WILLIAM SHAKSPEARE.

" I warrant thee, Euseby, the damp began not at the outside. A word in thy ear—Lucifer was thy tapster, I trow."

SIR THOMAS.

" Irreverent swine! hast no awe nor shame? Thou hast aggravated thy offence, William Shakspeare, by thy foul-mouthedness."

SIR SILAS.

" I must remind your worship, that he not only has committed this iniquity afore, but hath pawed the puddle he made, and relapsed into it after due caution and reproof. God forbid that what he spake against me, out of the gall of his proud stomach, should move me. I defy him, a low ignorant wretch, a rogue and vagabond, a thief and cut-throat, a . . .* monger and mutton-eater."

---

* Here the manuscript is blotted; but the probability is, that it was *fishmonger*, rather than *ironmonger*, fishmongers having always been notorious cheats and liars.

WILLIAM SHAKSPEARE.

" Your worship doth hear the learned clerk's testimony in my behalf. 'Out of the mouth of babes and sucklings—'"

SIR THOMAS.

" Silas! The youth has failings—a madcap; but he is pious."

WILLIAM SHAKSPEARE.

" Alas, no, sir! Would I were! But Sir Silas, like the prophet, came to curse and was forced to bless me, even me, a sinner, a mutton-eater!"

SIR THOMAS.

" Thou urgedst him. He beareth no ill-will towards thee. Thou knewedst, I suspect, that the blackness in his mouth proceeded from a natural cause."

WILLIAM SHAKSPEARE.

" The Lord is merciful! I was brought hither in jeopardy; I shall return in joy. Whether my innocence be declared or other-wise, my piety and knowledge will be forwarded and increased : for your worship will condescend, even from the judgment-seat, to enlighten the ignorant where a soul shall be saved or lost! And I, even I, may trespass a moment on your courtesy. I quail at the words *natural cause.*   Be there any such?"

SIR THOMAS.

" Youth! I never thought thee so staid. Thou hast, for these many months, been represented unto me as one dissolute and light, much given unto mummeries and mysteries, wakes and carousals, cudgel-fighters and mountebanks, and wanton women. They do also represent of thee—I hope it may be without foundation—that thou enactest the parts, not simply of foresters and fairies, girls in the green-sickness and friars, lawyers and outlaws, but likewise, having small reverence for station, of kings and queens, knights and privy-counsellors, in all their glory. It hath been whispered, moreover, and the testimony of these two witnesses doth appear in some measure to countenance and confirm it, that thou hast at divers times this last summer been seen and heard. alone, inasmuch as human eye may discover, on the narrow slip of greensward between the Avon and the chancel, distorting thy body like one possessed, and uttering strange language, like unto incantation. This, however, cometh not before me. Take heed! take heed unto thy ways : there are graver things in law even than homicide and deer-stealing."

SIR SILAS.

" And strong against him. Folks have been consumed at the stake for pettier felonies and upon weaker evidence."

SIR THOMAS.

" To that anon."

William Shakspeare did hold down his head, answering nought. And Sir Thomas spake again unto him, as one mild and fatherly, if so be that such a word may be spoken of a knight and parliament-man. And these are the words he spake:

" Reason and ruminate with thyself now. To pass over and pretermit the danger of representing the actions of the others, and mainly of lawyers and churchmen, the former of whom do pardon no offences, and the latter those only against God, having no warrant for more, canst thou believe it innocent to counterfeit kings and queens? Supposest thou that if the impression of their faces on a farthing be felonious and rope-worthy, the imitation of head and body, voice and bearing, plume and strut, crown and mantle, and every thing else that maketh them royal and glorious, be aught less? Perpend, young man, perpend! Consider who among inferior mortals shall imitate them becomingly? Dreamest thou they talk and act like checkmen at Banbury fair? How can thy shallow brain suffice for their vast conceptions? How darest thou say, as they do, hang this fellow — quarter that — flay — mutilate — stab —

shoot — press — hook — torture — burn alive? These are royalties. Who appointed thee to such office? The Holy Ghost? He alone can confer it; but when wert thou anointed?"

William was so zealous in storing up these verities, that he looked as though he were unconscious that the pouring-out was over. He started, which he had not done before, at the voice of Master Silas; but soon recovered his complacency, and smiled with much serenity at being called low-minded varlet.

" Low-minded varlet!" cried Master Silas, most contemptuously, " dost thou imagine that king calleth king, like thy chums, *filcher* and *fibber, whirligig* and *nincompoop?* Instead of this low vulgarity and sordid idleness, ending in nothing, they throw at one another such fellows as thee by the thousand, and when they have cleared the land, render God thanks and make peace."

Willy did now sigh out his ignorance of these matters; and he sighed, mayhap, too, at the recollection of the peril he had run into, and had ne'er a word on the nail.*

The bowels of Sir Thomas waxed tenderer and tenderer; and he opened his lips in this fashion:

" Stripling! I would now communicate unto thee, on finding thee docile and assentaneous, the instruction thou needest on the signification of the words *natural cause,* if thy duty towards thy neighbour had been first instilled into thee."

Whereupon Master Silas did interpose, for the dinner-hour was drawing nigh.

" We cannot do all at once," quoth he. " Coming out of order, it might harm him. Malt before hops, the world over, or the beer muddies."

But Sir Thomas was not to be pricked out of his form even by so shrewd a pricker; and, like unto one who heareth not, he continued to

* *On the nail* appears to be intended to express *ready payment.*

look most graciously on the homely vessel that stood ready to receive his wisdom:

" Thy mind," said he, " being unprepared for higher cogitations, and the groundwork and religious duty not being well rammer-beaten and flinted, I do pass over this supererogatory point, and inform thee rather, that bucks and swans and herons have something in their very names announcing them of knightly appertenance. And (God forfend that evil do ensue therefrom !) that a goose on the common, or a game-cock on the loft of cottager or villager, may be seized, bagged, and abducted, with far less offence to the laws. In a buck there is something so gainly and so grand, he treadeth the earth with such ease and such agility, he abstaineth from all other animals with such punctilious avoidance, one would imagine God created him when he created knighthood. In the swan there is such purity, such coldness is there in the element he inhabiteth, such solitude of station, that verily he doth remind.me of the

Virgin Queen herself. Of the heron I have less
to say, not having him about me; but I never
heard his lordly croak without the conceit that
it resembled a chancellor's or a primate's.

" I do perceive, William Shakspeare, thy
compunction and contrition."

WILLIAM SHAKSPEARE.

" I was thinking, may it please your worship, of the game-cock and the goose, having
but small notion of herons. This doctrine of
abduction, please your worship, hath been alway
inculcated by the soundest of our judges. Would
they had spoken on other points with the same
clearness.   How many unfortunates might
thereby have been saved from crossing the
Cordilleras!"*

* The Cordilleras are mountains, we know, running
through South America. Perhaps a pun was intended; or
possibly it might, in the age of Elizabeth, have been a vulgar term for *hanging*, although we find no trace of the expression in other books. We have no clue to guide us
here. It might be suggested that Shakspeare, who shines
little in geographical knowledge, fancied the Cordilleras to

SIR THOMAS.

" Ay, ay! they have been fain to fly the country at last, thither or elsewhere."

And then did Sir Thomas call unto him Master Silas, and say,

" Walk we into the bay-window.   And thou mayest come, Ephraim."

And when we were there together, I, Master Silas, and his worship, did his worship say unto the chaplain, but oftener looking towards me,

" I am not ashamed to avouch that it goeth against me to hang this young fellow, richly as the offence in its own nature doth deserve it, he talketh so reasonably; not indeed so reasonably, but so like unto what a reasonable man may listen to and reflect on. There is so much, too, of compassion for others in hard cases, and something so very near in semblance to innocence itself in that airy swing of lighthearted-

extend into North America, had convicts in his time been transported to those colonies. Certainly, many adventurers and desperate men went thither.

ness about him.   I cannot fix my eyes (as one would say) on the shifting and sudden *shade-and-shine*, which cometh back to me, do what I will, and mazes me in a manner, and blinks me."

At this juncture I was ready to fall upon the ground before his worship, and clasp his knees for Willy's pardon.   But he had so many points about him, that I feared to discompose 'em, and thus make bad worse.   Beside which, Master Silas left me but scanty space for good resolutions, crying,

" He may be committed, to save time.   Afterwards he may be sentenced to death, or he may not."

SIR THOMAS.

" 'Twere shame upon me were he not : 'twere indication that I acted unadvisedly in the commitment."

SIR SILAS.

" The penalty of the law may be commuted, if expedient, on application to the fountain of mercy in London."

SIR THOMAS.

" Maybe, Silas, those shall be standing round the fount of mercy who play in idleness and wantonness with its waters, and let them not flow widely, nor take their natural course. Dutiful gallants may encompass it, and it may linger among the flowers they throw into it, and never reach the parched lip on the way-side.

"These are homely thoughts—thoughts from a-field, thoughts for the study and housekeeper's room. But whenever I have given utterance unto them, as my heart hath often prompted me with beatings at the breast, my hearers seemed to bear towards me more true and kindly affection than my richest fancies and choicest phraseologies could purchase.

" 'Twere convenient to bethink thee, should any other great man's park have been robbed this season, no judge upon the bench will back my recommendation for mercy. And, indeed, how could I expect it? Things may soon be brought to such a pass that their lordships shall scarcely find three haunches each upon the circuit."

" Well, Sir!" quoth Master Silas, " you have a right to go on in your own way. Make him only give up the girl."

Here Sir Thomas reddened with righteous indignation, and answered,

" I cannot think it! such a stripling! poor, pennyless: it must be some one else."

And now Master Silas did redden in his turn redder than Sir Thomas, and first asked me,

" What the devil do you stare at?"

And then asked his worship,

" Who should it be if not the rogue?" and his lips turned as blue as a blue-bell.

Then Sir Thomas left the window, and again took his chair, and having stood so long on his legs, groaned upon it to ease him. His worship scowled with all his might, and looked exceedingly wroth and vengeful at the culprit, and said unto him,

" Harkye, knave! I have been conferring with my learned clerk and chaplain in what manner I may, with the least severity, rid the county (which thou disgracest) of thee."

William Shakspeare raised up his eyes, modestly and fearfully, and said slowly these few words, which, had they been a better and nobler man's, would deserve to be written in letters of gold. I, not having that art nor substance, do therefore write them in my largest and roundest character, and do leave space about 'em, according to their rank and dignity :

" Worshipful sir!

" A WORD IN THE EAR IS OFTEN AS GOOD AS A HALTER UNDER IT, AND SAVES THE GROAT."

" Thou discoursest well," said Sir Thomas, " but others can discourse well likewise : thou shalt avoid ; I am resolute."

WILLIAM SHAKSPEARE.

" I supplicate your honour to impart unto me, in your wisdom, the mode and means whereby I may surcease to be disgraceful to the county.

SIR THOMAS.

" I am not bloody-minded.

" First, thou shalt have the fairest and fullest examination.   Much hath been deposed against thee : something may come forth for thy advantage.   I will not thy death : thou shalt not die.

" The laws have loopholes, like castles, both to shoot from and to let folks down."

SIR SILAS.

" That pointed ear would look the better for paring, and that high forehead can hold many letters."

Whereupon did William, poor lad! turn deadly pale, but spake not.

Sir Thomas then abated a whit of his severity, and said, staidly :

" Testimony doth appear plain and positive against thee; nevertheless am I minded and prompted to aid thee myself, in disclosing and unfolding what thou couldst not of thine own wits, in furtherance of thine own defence.

" One witness is persuaded and assured of the evil spirit having been abroad, and the punt appeared unto him diversely from what it appeared unto the other."

WILLIAM SHAKSPEARE.

" If the evil spirit produced one appearance, he might have produced all, with deference to the graver judgment of your worship.

" If what seemed *punt* was *devil*, what seemed *buck* might have been *devil* too; nay, more easily, the horns being forthcoming.

" Thieves and reprobates do resemble him more nearly still; and it would be hard if he could not make free with their bodies, when he has their souls already."

SIR THOMAS.

" But, then, those voices! and thou thyself, Will Shakspeare !"

WILLIAM SHAKSPEARE.

" O might I kiss the hand of my deliverer, whose clear-sightedness throweth such manifest and plenary light upon my innocence !"

SIR THOMAS.

" How so ? What light, in God's name, have I thrown upon it as yet ?"

WILLIAM SHAKSPEARE.

" Oh ! those voices ! those faeries and spirits ! whence came they ? None can deal with 'em but the devil, the parson, and witches. And does not the devil oftentimes take the very form, features, and habiliments, of knights, and bishops, and other good men, to lead them into temptation and destroy them ? or to injure their good name, in failure of seduction ?

" He is sure of the wicked : he lets them go their ways out of hand.

" I think your worship once delivered some such observation, in more courtly guise, which

I would not presume to ape. If it was not your worship, it was our glorious lady the queen, or the wise Master Walsingham, or the great Lord Cecil. I may have marred and broken it, as sluts do a pancake, in the turning."

SIR THOMAS.

" Why! ay, indeed, I had occasion once to remark as much."

WILLIAM SHAKSPEARE.

" So have I heard in many places; although I was not present when Matthew Atterend fought about it, for the honour of Kineton hundred."

SIR THOMAS.

" Fought about it !"

WILLIAM SHAKSPEARE.

" As your honour recollects. Not but on other occasions he would have fought no less bravely for the queen."

SIR THOMAS.

" We must get thee through, were it only

F

for thy memory—the most precious gift among the mental powers that Providence hath bestowed upon us. I had half forgotten the thing myself. Thou mayest, in time, take thy satchel for London, and aid good old Master Holingshed.

"We must clear thee, Will! I am slow to surmise that there is blood upon thy hands!"

His worship's choler had all gone down again; and he sat as cool and comfortable as a man sitteth to be shaved. Then called he on Euseby Treen, and said—

"Euseby Treen! tell us whether thou observedst any thing unnoticed or unsaid by the last witness."

EUSEBY TREEN.

"One thing only, sir!

"When they had passed the water, an owlet hooted after them; and methought, if they had any fear of God before their eyes, they would have turned back, he cried so lustily."

WILLIAM SHAKSPEARE.

" Sir, I cannot forbear to take the owlet out of your mouth. He knocks them all on the head like so many mice. Likely story! One fellow hears him cry lustily, the other doth not hear him at all."

JOSEPH CARNABY.

" Not hear him! A body might have heard him at Barford or Sherbourne."

SIR THOMAS.

" Why didst not name him? Canst not answer me ?"

JOSEPH CARNABY.

" *He* doubted whether punt were punt — I doubted whether owlet were owlet, after Lucifer was away from the roll-call.

" We say, *speak the truth and shame the devil;* but shaming him is one thing, your honour, and facing him another! I have heard owlets, but never owlet like him."

WILLIAM SHAKSPEARE.

" The Lord be praised! All, at last, a-running to my rescue.

" Owlet, indeed! Your worship may have remembered in an ancient book — indeed, what book is so ancient that your worship doth not remember it? — a book printed by Doctor Faustus ——"

SIR THOMAS.

" Before he dealt with the devil?"

WILLIAM SHAKSPEARE.

" Not long before; it being the very book that made the devil think it worth his while to deal with him."

SIR THOMAS.

" What chapter thereof wouldst thou recall unto my recollection?"

WILLIAM SHAKSPEARE.

" That concerning owls, with the grim print afore it.

" Doctor Faustus, the wise doctor, who knew other than owls and owlets, knew the tempter in that form. Faustus was not your man for fancies and figments ; and he tells us that, to his certain knowledge, it was verily an owl's face that whispered so much mischief in the ear of our first parent.

" One plainly sees it, quoth Doctor Faustus, under that gravity which in human life we call dignity, but of which we read nothing in the Gospel. We despise the hangman, we detest the hanged ; and yet, saith Duns Scotus, could we turn aside the heavy curtain, or stand high enough a-tiptoe to peep through its chinks and crevices, we should perhaps find these two characters to stand justly among the most innocent in the drama. He who blinketh the eyes of the poor wretch about to die doeth it out of mercy ; those who preceded him, bidding him in the garb of justice to shed the blood of his fellow-man, had less or none. So they hedge well their own grounds, what care they ? For this do they catch at stakes and thorns, at quick and rotten . . ."

Here Master Silas interrupted the discourse of the devil's own doctor, delivered and printed by him before he was the devil's, to which his worship had listened very attentively and delightedly. But Master Silas could keep his temper no longer, and cried fiercely, " Seditious sermonizer! hold thy peace, or thou shalt answer for't before convocation."

SIR THOMAS.

" Silas! thou dost not approve then the doctrine of this Doctor Duns?"

SIR SILAS.

" Heretical Rabbi!"

WILLIAM SHAKSPEARE.

" *If two of a trade can never agree,* yet surely two of a name may."

SIR SILAS.

" Who dares call me heretical? who dares call me rabbi? who dares call me Scotus? Spider! spider! yea, thou hast one corner left: I espy thee; and my broom shall reach thee yet." . . .

WILLIAM SHAKSPEARE.

" I perceive that Master Silas doth verily believe I have been guilty of suborning the witnesses, at least the last, the best man (if any difference) of the two. No, sir, no. If my family and friends have united their wits and money for this purpose, be the crime of perverted justice on their heads! They injure whom they intended to serve. Improvident men! if the young may speak thus of the elderly; could they imagine to themselves that your worship was to be hoodwinked and led astray?"

SIR THOMAS.

" No man shall ever dare to hoodwink me, to lead me astray, no, nor lead me anywise. Powerful defence! Heyday! Sit quiet, Master Treen!—Euseby Treen! dost hear me? Clench thy fist again, sirrah! and I clap thee in the stocks.

" Joseph Carnaby! do not scratch thy breast nor thy pate before me."

Now Joseph had not only done that in his wrath, but had unbuckled his leathern garter, fit instrument for strife and blood, and peradventure would have smitten, had not the knight, with magisterial authority, interposed.

His worship said unto him gravely, " Joseph Carnaby! Joseph Carnaby! hast thou never read the words ' *Put up thy sword?*'"

" Subornation! your worship!" cried Master Joe. " The fellow hath ne'er a shilling in leather or till, and many must go to suborn one like me."

" I do believe it of thee," said Sir Thomas; " but patience, man! patience! he rather tended towards exculpating thee. Ye have far to walk for dinner; ye may depart."

They went accordingly.

Then did Sir Thomas say, " These are hot men, Silas!"

And Master Silas did reply unto him, " These are brands that would set fire to the bulrushes in the mill-pool. I know these twain for quiet folks, having coursed with them over Wincott."

Sir Thomas then said unto William, " It behoveth thee to stand clear of yon Joseph, unless when thou mayest call to thy aid the Matthew Atterend thou speakest of. He did then fight valiantly, eh ? "

WILLIAM SHAKSPEARE.

" His cause fought valiantly; his fist but seconded it. He won; proving the golden words to be no property of our lady's, although her highness hath never disclaimed them."

SIR THOMAS.

" What art thou saying ? "

WILLIAM SHAKSPEARE.

" So I heard from a preacher at Oxford, who had preached at Easter in the chapel-royal of Westminster."   .

SIR THOMAS.

" Thou ! why how could that happen? Oxford ! chapel-royal !

WILLIAM SHAKSPEARE.

" And to whom I said (your worship will forgive my forwardness), *I have the honour, sir, to live within two measured miles of the very Sir Thomas Lucy who spake that.* And I vow I said it without any hope or belief that he would invite me, as he did, to dine with him thereupon."

SIR THOMAS.

" There be nigh upon three miles betwixt this house and Stratford bridge-end.

WILLIAM SHAKSPEARE.

" I dropt a mile in my pride and exultation, God forgive me ! I would not conceal my fault."

SIR THOMAS.

" Wonderful! that a preacher so learned as to preach before majesty in the chapel-royal, should not have caught thee tripping over a whole lawful mile—a good third of the distance between my house and the cross roads. This is incomprehensible in a scholar."

WILLIAM SHAKSPEARE.

" God willed that he should become my teacher, and, in the bowels of his mercy, hid my shame."

SIR THOMAS.

" How camest thou into the converse of such eminent and ghostly men ?"

WILLIAM SHAKSPEARE.

" How, indeed ! Every thing against me."

He sighed, and entered into a long discourse, which Master Silas would at sundry times have interrupted, but that Sir Thomas more than once frowned upon him, even as he had frowned heretofore on young Will, who thus began and continued his narration.

" Hearing the preacher preach at Saint Mary's (for being about my father's business on Saturday, and not choosing to be a-horseback on Sundays, albeit time-pressed, I footed it to Oxford for my edification on the Lord's day, leaving the sorrel with Master Hal Webster of the *Tankard and Unicorn*)—hearing him preach, as I was saying, before the University in St. Mary's church, and hearing him use moreover the very words that Matthew fought about, I was impatient (God forgive me!) for the end and consummation, and I thought I never should hear those precious words that ease every man's heart, ' *Now to conclude.*' However, come they did. I hurried out among the foremost, and thought the congratulations of the other doctors and dons would last for ever. He walked sharply off, and few cared to keep his pace; for they are lusty men mostly; and spiteful bad women had breathed * in the faces

* In that age there was prevalent a sort of cholera, on which Fracastorius, half a century before, wrote a Latin poem, employing the graceful nymphs of Homer and Hesiod, somewhat disguised, in the drudgery of pounding certain barks and minerals. An article in the Impeachment of Cardinal Wolsey, accuses him of breathing in the king's face, knowing that he was affected with this cholera. It was a great assistant to the Reformation, by removing some of the most vigorous champions that opposed it. In the Holy College it was followed by the *sweating sickness,* which thinned it very sorely; and several even of God's

of some among them, or the gowns had got between their legs. For my part, I was not to be balked : so, tripping on aside him, I looked in his face askance. Whether he misgave, or how, he turned his eyes downward. No matter—have him I would. I licked my lips and smacked them loud and smart, and, scarcely venturing to nod, I gave my head such a sort of motion as dace and roach give an angler's quill when they begin to bite. And this fairly hooked him."

" ' Young gentleman ! ' said he, ' where is your gown ?'

" ' Reverend sir !' said I, ' I am unworthy to wear one.'

" ' A proper youth, nevertheless, and might-ily well-spoken !' he was pleased to say.

" ' Your reverence hath given me heart,

vicegerents were laid under tribulation by it. Among the chambers of the Vatican it hung for ages, and it crowned the labours of Pope Leo XII., of blessed memory, with a crown somewhat uneasy.

which failed me,' was my reply. ' Ah! your reverence! those words about the devil were spicy words; but, under favour, I do know the brook-side they sprang and flowered by. 'Tis just where it runs into Avon; 'tis called Hog-brook.'

"' Right!' quoth he, putting his hand gently on my shoulder; ' but if I had thought it needful to say so in my sermon, I should have affronted the seniors of the University, since many claim them, and some peradventure would fain transpose them into higher places, and, giving up all right and title to them, would accept in lieu thereof the poor recompense of a mitre.'

" I wished (unworthy wish for a Sunday!) I had Matthew Atterend in the midst of them. He would have given them skulls mitre-fashioned, if mitres are cloven now as we see them on ancient monuments. Matt is your milliner for gentles, who think no more harm of purloining rich saws in a mitre, than lane-born boys do of embezzling hazle-nuts in a woollen cap. I did not venture to expound or suggest my thoughts, but feeling my choler rise higher and higher, I craved permission to make my obeisance and depart."

" ' Where dost thou lodge, young man?' said the preacher.

" ' At the public,' said I, ' where my father customarily lodgeth. There, too, is a mitre of the old fashion, swinging on the sign-post in the middle of the street.'

" ' Respectable tavern enough!' quoth the reverend doctor; ' and worthy men do turn in there, even quality—Master Davenant, Master Powel, Master Whorwood, aged and grave men. But taverns are Satan's chapels, and are always well attended on the Lord's day, to twit him. Hast thou no friend in such a city as Oxford?'

" ' Only the landlady of the Mitre,' said I.

" ' A comely woman,' quoth he, ' but too young for business by half.

" ' Stay thou with me to-day, and fare fru-
gally, but safely.

" ' What may thy name be, and where is
thy abode?'

" ' William Shakspeare, of Stratford-upon-
Avon, at your service, sir.'

" ' And welcome,' said he; ' thy father ere
now hath bought our college wool.   A truly
good man we ever found him; and I doubt not
he hath educated his son to follow him in his
paths.   There is in the blood of man, as in the
blood of animals, that which giveth the temper
and disposition.   These require nurture and
culture.   But what nurture will turn flint-stones
into garden mould? or what culture rear cab-
bages in the quarries of Hedington Hill?   To
be well born is the greatest of all God's primary
blessings, young man, and there are many well
born among the poor and needy.   Thou art not
of the indigent and destitute, who have great
temptations; thou art not of the wealthy and
affluent, who have greater still.   God hath

placed thee, William Shakspeare, in that pleasant island, on one side whereof are the syrens, on the other the harpies, but inhabiting the coasts on the wider continent, and unable to make their talons felt, or their voices heard by thee. Unite with me in prayer and thanksgiving for the blessings thus vouchsafed. We must not close the heart when the finger of God would touch it. Enough, if thou sayest only, *My soul, praise thou the Lord!*' "

Sir Thomas said, "*Amen!*" Master Silas was mute for the moment, but then quoth he, " I can say amen too, in the proper place."

The knight of Charlecote, who appeared to have been much taken with this conversation, then interrogated Willy:

" What farther might have been thy discourse with the doctor? or did he discourse at all at trencher-time? Thou must have been very much abashed to sit down at table with one who weareth a pure lamb-skin across his shoulder, and moreover a pink hood."

WILLIAM SHAKSPEARE.

" Faith! was I, your honour! and could neither utter nor gulp."

SIR THOMAS.

" These are good signs.   Thou hast not lost all grace."

WILLIAM SHAKSPEARE.

" With the encouragement of Doctor Glaston——"

SIR THOMAS.

" And was it Dr. Glaston?"

WILLIAM SHAKSPEARE.

" Said I not so?"

SIR THOMAS.

" The learnedst clerk in Christendom! a very Friar Bacon! The pope offered a hundred marks in Latin to who should eviscerate or evirate him — poisons very potent, whereat the Italians are handy — so apostolic and desperate a doctor is Doctor Glaston! so acute in his quiddities, and so resolute in his bearing! He knows the dark arts, but stands aloof from them.   Prythee, what were his words unto thee ?"

WILLIAM SHAKSPEARE.

" Manna, sir, manna! pure from the desert!"

SIR THOMAS.

" Ay, but what spake he? for most sermons are that, and likewise many conversations after dinner."

WILLIAM SHAKSPEARE.

" He spake of the various races and qualities of men, as before stated; but chiefly on the elect and reprobate, and how to distinguish and know them."

SIR THOMAS.

" Did he go so far?"

WILLIAM SHAKSPEARE.

" He told me, that by such discussion he should say enough to keep me constantly out of evil company."

SIR THOMAS.

" See there! see there! and yet thou art come before me!   Can nothing warn thee?"

WILLIAM SHAKSPEARE.

" I dare not dissemble, nor feign, nor hold aught back, although it be to my confusion. As well may I speak at once the whole truth; for your worship could find it out if I abstained."

SIR THOMAS.

" Ay, that I should indeed, and shortly. But, come now, I am sated of thy follies and roguish tricks, and yearn after the sound doctrine of that pious man. What expounded the grave Glaston upon signs and tokens whereby ye shall be known?"

WILLIAM SHAKSPEARE.

" Wonderful things! things beyond belief! ' There be certain men,' quoth he ——"

SIR THOMAS.

" He began well. This promises. But why canst not thou go on?"

WILLIAM SHAKSPEARE.

" ' There be certain men, who, rubbing one corner of the eye, do see a peacock's feather at the other, and even fire. We know, William, what that fire is, and whence it cometh. Those wicked men, William, all have their marks upon them, be it only a corn, or a wart, or a mole, or a hairy ear, or a toe-nail turned inward. Sufficient, and more than sufficient! He knoweth his own by less tokens. There is not one of them that doth not sweat at some secret sin committed, or some inclination toward it unsnaffled.

" ' Certain men are there, likewise, who venerate so little the glorious works of the Creator, that I myself have known them to sneeze at the sun! Sometimes it was against their will, and they would gladly have checked it had they been able; but they were forced to shew what they are. In our carnal state we say, *What is one against numbers?* In another, we shall truly say, *What are numbers against one?* '"

Sir Thomas did ejaculate, " *Amen! Amen!*" And then his lips moved silently, piously, and quickly; and then said he, audibly and loudly,

" *And make us at last true Israelites !*"

After which he turned to young Willy, and said anxiously,

" Hast thou more, lad ? give us it while the Lord strengtheneth."

" Sir," answered Willy, " although I thought it no trouble, on my return to the *Mitre*, to write down every word I could remember, and although few did then escape me, yet at this present I can bring to mind but scanty sentences, and those so stray and out of order that they would only prove my incapacity for sterling wisdom, and my incontinence of spiritual treasure."

SIR THOMAS.

" Even that sentence hath a twang of the doctor in it. Nothing is so sweet as humility. The mountains may descend, but the valleys cannot rise. Every man should know himself. Come, repeat what thou canst. I would fain have three or four more heads."

WILLIAM SHAKSPEARE.

" I know not whether I can give your worship more than one other. Let me try. It was
when Doctor Glaston was discoursing on the
protection the wise and powerful should afford
to the ignorant and weak :—

" ' In the earlier ages of mankind, your
Greek and Latin authors inform you, there
went forth sundry worthies, men of might, to
deliver, not wandering damsels, albeit for those
likewise they had stowage, but low-conditioned
men, who fell under the displeasure of the
higher, and groaned in thraldom and captivity.
And these mighty ones were believed to have
done such services to poor humanity, that their
memory grew greater than they, as shadows do
than substances at day-fall. And the sons and
grandsons of the delivered did laud and magnify those glorious names ; and some in gratitude, and some in tribulation, did ascend the
hills, which appeared unto them as altars be-
strown with flowers and herbage for heaven's

acceptance. And many did go far into the quiet groves, under lofty trees, looking for whatever was mightiest and most protecting. And in such places did they cry aloud unto the mighty, who had left them,

"'*Return! return! help us! help us! be blessed! for ever blessed!*'

"'Vain men! but, had they stayed there, not evil. Out of gratitude, purest gratitude, rose idolatry. For the devil sees the fairest, and soils it.

"'In these our days, methinks, whatever other sins we may fall into, such idolatry is the least dangerous. For, neither on the one side is there much disposition for gratitude, nor on the other much zeal to deliver the innocent and oppressed. Even this deliverance, although a merit, and a high one, is not the highest. Forgiveness is beyond it. Forgive, or ye shall not be forgiven. This ye may do every day; for, if ye find not offences, ye feign them; and surely ye may remove your own work, if ye may remove another's. To rescue requires more thought and wariness: learn then the easier lesson first. Afterwards, when ye rescue any from another's violence, or from his own (which oftentimes is more dangerous, as the enemies are within not only the penetrails of his house but of his heart), bind up his wounds before ye send him on his way. Should ye at any time overtake the erring, and resolve to deliver him up, I will tell you whither to conduct him. Conduct him to his Lord and Master, whose household he hath left. It is better to consign him to Christ his Saviour than to man his murderer: it is better to bid him live than to bid him die. The one word our Teacher and Preserver said, the other our enemy and destroyer. Bring him back again, the stray, the lost one! bring him back, not with clubs and cudgels, not with halberts and halters, but generously and gently, and with the linking of the arm. In this posture shall God above smile upon ye: in this posture of yours he shall recognise again his beloved Son upon earth. Do ye likewise, and depart in peace.'"

William had ended, and there was silence in the hall for some time after, when Sir Thomas said,

" He spake unto somewhat mean persons, who may do it without disparagement. I look for authority, I look for doctrine, and find none yet. If he could not have drawn us out a thread or two from the coat of an apostle, he might have given us a smack of Augustin, or a sprig of Basil. Our older sermons are headier than these, Master Silas! our new beer is the sweeter and clammier, and wants more spice. The doctor hath seasoned his with pretty wit enough, to do him justice, which in a sermon is never out of place; for if there be the bane there likewise is the antidote.

" What dost thou think about it, Master Silas?"

SIR SILAS.

" I would not give ten farthings for ten folios of such sermons."

WILLIAM SHAKSPEARE.

" These words, Master Silas, will oftener be quoted than any others of thine; but rarely (do I suspect) as applicable to Doctor Glaston. I must stick unto his gown. I must declare that, to my poor knowledge, many have been raised to the bench of bishops for less wisdom, and worse than is contained in the few sentences I have been commanded by authority to recite. No disparagement to any body! I know, Master Silas, and multitudes bear witness, that thou above most art a dead hand at a sermon."

SIR SILAS.

" Touch my sermons, wilt dare? "

WILLIAM SHAKSPEARE.

" Nay, Master Silas, be not angered: it is courage enough to hear them."

SIR THOMAS.

" Now, Silas, hold thy peace and rest contented. He hath excused himself unto thee, throwing in a compliment far above his station, and not unworthy of Rome or Florence. I did not think him so ready. Our Warwickshire lads are fitter for football than courtesies; and, sooth to say, not only the inferior."

His worship turned from Master Silas towards William, and said, " Brave Willy, thou hast given us our bitters; we are ready now for any thing solid. What hast left ? "

WILLIAM SHAKSPEARE.

" Little or nothing, sir."

SIR THOMAS.

" Well, give us that little or nothing."

William Shakspeare was obedient to the commands of Sir Thomas, who had spoken thus kindly unto him, and had deigned to cast at him from his *lordly dish* (as the Psalmist hath it) a fragment of facetiousness.

WILLIAM SHAKSPEARE.

" Alas, sir! may I repeat it without offence, it not being doctrine but admonition, and meant for me only ? "

" Speak it the rather for that," quoth Sir Thomas.

Then did William give utterance to the words of the preacher, not indeed in his sermon at St. Mary's, but after dinner.

" ' Lust seizeth us in youth, ambition in mid-life, avarice in old age; but vanity and pride are the besetting sins that drive the angels from our cradle, pamper us with luscious and most unwholesome food, ride our first stick with us, mount our first horse with us, wake with us in the morning, dream with us in the night, and never at any time abandon us. In this world, beginning with pride and vanity, we are delivered over from tormentor to tormentor, until the worst tormentor of all taketh absolute possession of us for ever, seizing us at the mouth of the grave, enchaining us in his own dark dungeon, standing at the door, and laughing at our cries. But the Lord, out of his infinite mercy, hath placed in the hand of every man the helm to steer his course by, pointing it out with his finger, and giving him strength as well as knowledge to pursue it.

" ' William! William! there is in the moral straits a current from right to wrong, but no reflux from wrong to right; for which destination we must hoist our sails aloft and ply our oars incessantly, or night and the tempest will overtake us, and we shall shriek out in vain from the billows, and irrecoverably sink.' "

" Amen! " cried Sir Thomas most devoutly, sustaining his voice long and loud.

" Open that casement, good Silas! the day is sultry for the season of the year: it approacheth unto noontide. The room is close, and those blue flies do make a strange hubbub."

WILLIAM SHAKSPEARE.

" In troth do they, sir; they come from the kitchen, and do savour woundily of roast goose! And, methinks ——"

SIR THOMAS.

" What bethinkest thou?"

WILLIAM SHAKSPEARE.

" The fancy of a moment—a light and vain one."

SIR THOMAS.

" Thou relievest me; speak it?"

WILLIAM SHAKSPEARE.

" How could the creatures cast their coarse rank odour thus far? even into thy presence! A noble and spacious hall! Charlecote, in my mind, beats Warwick Castle, and challenges Kenilworth."

SIR THOMAS.

" The hall is well enough : I must say it is a noble hall—a hall for a queen to sit down in. And I stuffed an arm-chair with horse-hair on purpose, feathers over it, swan-down over them again, and covered it with scarlet cloth of Bruges, five crowns the short ell. But her highness came not hither ; she was taken short; she had a tongue in her ear."

WILLIAM SHAKSPEARE.

" Where all is spring, all is buzz and murmur."

SIR THOMAS.

" Quaint and solid as the best yew-hedge.
I marvel at thee. A knight might have spoken
it under favour. They stopped her at Warwick—to see what? two old towers that don't
match,* and a portcullis that (people say)

* Sir Thomas seems to have been jealous of these two
towers, certainly the finest in England. If Warwick Castle
could borrow the windows from Kenilworth, it would be
complete. The knight is not very courteous on its hospi-
tality. He may, perhaps, have experienced it, as Garrick
and Quin did under the present occupant's grandfather, on
whom the title of Earl of Warwick was conferred for the
eminent services he had rendered to his country as one of
the lords of the bedchamber to his Majesty George the
Second. The verses of Garrick on his invitation and visit
are remembered by many. Quin's are less known:

" He shewed us Guy's pot, but the soup he forgot;
 Not a meal did his lordship allow,
 Unless we gnaw'd o'er the blade-bone of the boar,
  Or the rib of the famous *Dun Cow.*

" When Nevile the great Earl of Warwick lived here,
 Three oxen for breakfast were slain,
 And strangers invited to sports and good cheer,
  And invited again and again.

opens only upon fast-days. Charlecote Hall, I could have told her sweet highness, was built by those Lucies who came over with Julius Cesar and William the Conqueror, with cross and scallop-shell on breast and beaver."

" But, *honest Willy !?* "——-

Such were the very words; I wrote them down with two signs in the margent; one a mark of admiration, as thus (!), the other of interrogation (so we call it) as thus (?)"

" But, honest Willy, I would fain hear more," quoth he, " about the learned Doctor Glaston. He seemeth to be a man after God's own heart."

> " This earl is in purse or in spirit so low,
>   That he with no oxen will feed 'em ;
>   And all of the former great doings we know
>   Is, he gives us a book and we read 'em."

GARRICK.

> " *Stale* peers are but tough morsels, and 'twere well
>   If we had found the *fresh* more eatable :
>   Garrick ! I do not say 'twere well for *him*,
>   For we had pluck'd the plover limb from limb."

QUIN.

G 2

WILLIAM SHAKSPEARE.

" Ay is he!   Never doth he sit down to dinner but he readeth first a chapter of the Revelations; and if he tasteth a pound of butter at Carfax, he saith a grace long enough to bring an appetite for a baked bull's *... zle. If this be not after God's own heart, I know not what is."

SIR THOMAS.

" I would fain confer with him, but that Oxford lieth afar· off—a matter of thirty miles, I hear. I might, indeed, write unto him : but our Warwickshire pens are mighty broad-nibbed ; and there is a something in this plaguy ink of ours sadly ropy——"

---

* Another untoward blot ! but leaving no doubt of the word. The only doubt is, whether he meant the *muzzle* of the animal itself, or one of those leathern muzzles which are often employed to coerce the violence of ferocious animals. In besieged cities men have been reduced to such extremities. But the *muzzle*, in this place, we suspect, would more properly be called the *blinker*, which is often put upon bulls in pastures when they are vicious.

" I fear there is!" quoth Willy.

" And I should scorn," continued his worship, " to write otherwise than in a fine Italian character to the master of a college near in dignity to knighthood."

WILLIAM SHAKSPEARE.

" Worshipful sir! is there no other way of communicating but by person, or writing, or messages?"

SIR THOMAS.

" I will consider and devise. At present I can think of none so satisfactory."

And now did the great clock over the gateway strike. And Bill Shakspeare did move his lips, even as Sir Thomas had moved his erewhile in ejaculating. And when he had wagged them twice or thrice after the twelve strokes of the clock were over, again he ejaculated with voice also, saying,

" Mercy upon us! how the day wears! Twelve strokes! Might I retire, please your worship, into the chapel for about three quarters of an hour, and perform the service* as ordained ?"

Before Sir Thomas could give him leave or answer, did Sir Silas cry aloud,

" He would purloin the chalice, worth forty-eight shillings, and melt it down in the twinkling of an eye, he is so crafty."

But the knight was more reasonable, and said reprovingly,

" There now, Silas ! thou talkest widely, and verily in malice, if there be any in thee."

" Try him," answered Master Silas ; " I don't

---

* This would countenance the opinion of those who are inclined to believe that Shakspeare was a Roman Catholic. His hatred and contempt of priests, which are demonstrated wherever he has introduced them, may have originated from the unfairness of Silas Gough. Nothing of that kind, we may believe, had occurred to him from friars and monks, whom he treats respectfully and kindly, perhaps in return for some such services to himself as Friar Lawrence had bestowed on Romeo, or rather less; for Shakspeare was grateful. The words quoted by him from some sermon, now lost, prove him no friend to the filchings and swindling of popery.

kneel where he does. Could he have but his wicked will of me he would chop my legs off, as he did the poor buck's."

SIR THOMAS.

" No, no, no; he hath neither guile nor revenge in him. We may let him have his way, now that he hath taken the right one."

SIR SILAS.

" Popery! sheer popery! strong as hartshorn! Your papists keep these outlandish hours for their masses and mummery. Surely we might let God alone at twelve o'clock! Have we no bowels ?"

WILLIAM SHAKSPEARE.

" Gracious sir! I do not urge it; and the time is now past by some minutes."

SIR THOMAS.

" Art thou popishly inclined, William ?"

WILLIAM SHAKSPEARE.

" Sir, I am not popishly inclined : I am not inclined to pay tribute of coin or understanding to those who rush forward with a pistol at my breast, crying, ' *Stand, or you are a dead man.*' I have but one guide in faith—a powerful, an almighty one. He will not suffer to waste away and vanish the faith for which he died. He hath chosen in all countries pure hearts for its depositaries; and I would rather take it from a friend and neighbour, intelligent and righteous, and rejecting lucre, than from some foreigner educated in the pride of cities or in the moroseness of monasteries, who sells me what Christ gave me, his own flesh and blood.

" I can repeat by heart what I read above a year agone, albeit I cannot bring to mind the title of the book in which I read it. These are the words.

" 'The most venal and sordid of all the superstitions that have swept and darkened our globe, may, indeed, like African locusts, have consumed the green corn in very extensive regions, and may return periodically to consume it; but the strong unwearied labourer who sowed it hath alway sown it in other places less exposed to such devouring pestilences. Those cunning men who formed to themselves the gorgeous plan of universal dominion, were aware that they had a better chance of establishing it than brute ignorance or brute force could supply, and that soldiers and their pay-masters were subject to other and powerfuller fears than the transitory ones of war and invasion. What they found in heaven they seized; what they wanted they forged.

" ' And so long as there is vice and ignorance in the world; so long as fear is a passion, their dominion will prevail; but their dominion is not, and never shall be, universal. Can we wonder that it is so general? can we wonder that any thing is wanting to give it authority and effect, when every learned, every prudent, every powerful, every ambitious man in Europe, for above a thousand years, united in the league to consolidate it?

" The old dealers in the shambles, where

Christ's body is exposed for sale, in convenient marketable slices,* have not covered with blood and filth the whole pavement. Beautiful usages are remaining still — kinder affections, radiant hopes, and ardent aspirations!

" ' It is a comfortable thing to reflect, as they do, and as we may do unblamably, that we are uplifting to our Guide and Maker the same incense of the heart, and are uttering the very words, which our dearest friends in all quarters of the earth, nay in heaven itself, are offering to the throne of grace at the same moment.

" ' Thus are we together through the immensity of space. What are these bodies? Do *they* unite us? No; they keep us apart and asunder even while we touch. Realms and oceans, worlds and ages, open before two spirits bent

---

* It is a pity that the old divines should have indulged, as they often did, in such images as this. Some readers in search of argumentative subtility, some in search of sound Christianity, some in search of pure English undefiled, have gone through with them; and their labours (however heavy) have been well repaid.

on heaven. What a choir surrounds us when we resolve to live unitedly and harmoniously in Christian faith !'"

SIR THOMAS.

" Now, Silas, what sayest thou ?"

SIR SILAS.

" Ignorant fool !"

WILLIAM SHAKSPEARE.

" Ignorant fools are bearable, Master Silas ! your wise ones are the worst."

SIR THOMAS.

"Prythee no bandying of loggerheads."

WILLIAM SHAKSPEARE.

" Or else what mortal man shall say
Whose shins may suffer in the fray."

SIR THOMAS.

" Thou reasonest aptly and timest well. And surely being now in so rational and religious a frame of mind, thou couldst recall to memory a section or head or two of the sermon holden at Saint Mary's. It would do thee and us as much good as *Lighten our darkness,* or *Forasmuch as it hath pleased;* and somewhat less than three quarters of an hour (maybe less than one quarter) sufficeth."

SIR SILAS.

" Or he hangs without me.   I am for dinner in half the time."

SIR THOMAS.

" Silas! Silas! he hangeth not with thee or without thee."

SIR SILAS.

" He thinketh himself a clever fellow : but he (look ye) is the cleverest that gets off."

" I hold quite the contrary," quoth Will Shakspeare, winking at Master Silas, from the comfort and encouragement he had just received touching the hanging.

And Master Silas had his answer ready, and shewed that he was more than a match for poor Willy in wit and poetry.

He answered thus :—

" If winks are wit,
Who wanteth it ?

Thou hadst other bolts to kill bucks withal. In wit, sirrah, thou art a mere child."

WILLIAM SHAKSPEARE.

" Little dogs are jealous of children, great ones fondle them."

SIR THOMAS.

" An that were written in the Apocrypha, in the very teeth of Bel and the Dragon, it could not be truer. I have witnessed it with my own eyes over and over.

SIR SILAS.

" He will take this for wit, likewise, now the arms of Lucy do seal it."

SIR THOMAS.

" Silas, they may stamp wit, they may further wit, they may send wit into good company, but not make it."

WILLIAM SHAKSPEARE.

" Behold my wall of defence!"

SIR SILAS.

" An thou art for walls, I have one for thee from Oxford, pithy and apposite, sound and solid, and trimmed up becomingly, as a collar of brawn with a crown of rosemary, or a boar's head with a lemon in the mouth."

WILLIAM SHAKSPEARE.

" Egad, Master Silas ! those are your walls for lads to climb over, an they were higher than Babel's."

SIR SILAS.

" Have at thee !

> " Thou art a wall
>   To make the ball
>   Rebound from.

> " Thou hast a back
>   For beadle's crack
>   To sound from, to sound from.

The foolishest dolts are the ground-plot of the most wit, as the idlest rogues are of the most industry. Even thou hast brought wit down from Oxford. And before a thief is hanged, parliament must make laws, attorneys must engross them, printers stamp and publish them, hawkers cry them, judges expound them, juries weigh and measure them with offences, then executioners carry them into effect.   The farmer hath already sown, the hemp, the ropemaker hath twisted it; sawyers saw the timber, carpenters tack together the shell, grave-diggers delve the earth.   And all this truly for fellows like unto thee!"

WILLIAM SHAKSPEARE.

" Whom a God came down from heaven to save!"

SIR THOMAS.

" Silas! he hangeth not. William! I must have the heads of the sermon, six or seven of 'em: thou hast whetted my appetite keenly. How! dost duck thy pate into thy hat? nay, nay, that is proper and becoming at church; we need not such solemnity. Repeat unto us the setting forth at Saint Mary's."

Whereupon did William Shakspeare entreat of Master Silas that he would help him in his ghostly endeavours, by repeating what he called the *preliminary* prayer; which prayer I find no where in our ritual, and do suppose it to be one of those Latin supplications used in our learned universities now or erewhile.

I am afeard it hath not the approbation of the strictly orthodox, for inasmuch as Master Silas at such entreaty did close his teeth against it, and with teeth thus closed did say, Athanasius-wise, " Go and be damned !"

Bill was not disheartened, but said he hoped better, and began thus :—

" ' My brethren !' said the preacher, ' or rather let me call you my children, such is my age confronted with yours, for the most part,— my children, then, and my brethren, (for here are both,) believe me, killing is forbidden.' "

SIR THOMAS.

" This, not being delivered unto us from the pulpit by the preacher himself, we may look into. Sensible man! shrewd reasoner! what a stroke against deer-stealers! how full of truth and ruth! Excellent discourse!"

WILLIAM SHAKSPEARE.

" The last part was the best."

SIR THOMAS.

" I always find it so. The softest of the cheesecake is left in the platter when the crust is eaten.   He kept the best bit for the last, then?   He pushed it under the salt, eh?   He told thee——"

WILLIAM SHAKSPEARE.

" Exactly so."

SIR THOMAS.

" What was it?"

WILLIAM SHAKSPEARE.

" ' Ye shall not kill.'

SIR THOMAS.

" How! did he run in a circle like a hare? One of his mettle should break cover and off across the country, like a fox or hart."

WILLIAM SHAKSPEARE.

" ' And yet ye kill time when ye can, and are uneasy when ye cannot.'

Whereupon did Sir Thomas say aside unto himself, but within my hearing,

" Faith and troth! he must have had a head in at the window here one day or other."

WILLIAM SHAKSPEARE.

" ' This sin cryeth unto the Lord.'

SIR THOMAS.

" He was wrong there. It is not one of those that cry: mortal sins cry. Surely he could not have fallen into such an error! it must be thine : thou misunderstoodest him."

WILLIAM SHAKSPEARE.

" Mayhap, sir! A great heaviness came over me: I was oppressed in spirit, and did feel as one awakening from a dream."

SIR THOMAS.

" Godlier men than thou art do often feel the right hand of the Lord upon their heads in like manner. It followeth contrition, and precedeth conversion. Continue."

WILLIAM SHAKSPEARE.

" ' My brethren and children,' said the

teacher, ' whenever ye want to kill time call God to the chase, and bid the angels blow the horn; and thus ye are sure to kill time to your heart's content.   And ye may feast another day, and another after that...' "

Then said Master Silas unto me, concernedly,

" This is the mischief-fullest of all the devil's imps, to talk in such wise at a quarter past twelve !"

But William went straight on, not hearing him,

" ' Upon what ye shall in such pursuit have brought home with you.   Whereas, if ye go alone, or two or three together, nay, even if ye go in thick and gallant company, and yet pro-vide not that these be with ye, my word for it, and a powerfuller word than mine, ye shall return to your supper tired and jaded, and rest little when ye want to rest most.' "

" Hast no other head of the Doctor's ?" quoth Sir Thomas.

" Verily none," replied Willy, " of the

morning's discourse, saving the last words of it, which, with God's help, I shall always remember."

" Give us them, give us them," said Sir Thomas.

" He wants doctrine; he wants authority; his are grains of millet; grains for unfledged doves; but they are sound, except the *crying*.

" Deliver unto us the last words; for the last of the preacher, as of the hanged, are usually the best."

Then did William repeat the concluding words of the discourse, being these:

" ' As years are running past us, let us throw something on them which they cannot shake off in the dust and hurry of the world, but must carry with them to that great year of all, whereunto the lesser of this mortal life do tend and are subservient.' "

Sir Thomas, after a pause, and after having bent his knee under the table, as though there had been the church-cushion, said unto us,

" Here he spake *through a glass, darkly,*
as blessed Paul hath it."

Then turning towards Willy,

" And nothing more?"

" Nothing but the *glory,*" quoth Willy;
" at which there is alway such a clatter of
feet upon the floor, and creaking of benches,
and rustling of gowns, and bustle of bonnets,
and justle of cushions, and dust of mats, and
treading of toes, and punching of elbows, from
the spitefuller, that one wishes to be fairly out
of it, after the scramble for *the peace of God*
is at an end."

Sir Thomas threw himself back upon his
arm-chair, and exclaimed in wonderment,
" How !"

WILLIAM SHAKSPEARE.

" ... And in the midst of the service again,
were it possible. For nothing is painfuller than
to have the pail shaken off the head when it is
brim-full of the waters of life, and we are
walking staidly under it."

SIR THOMAS.

" Had the learned Doctor preached again in the evening, pursuing the thread of his discourse, he might, peradventure, have made up the deficiences I find in him."

WILLIAM SHAKSPEARE.

" He had not that opportunity."

SIR THOMAS.

" The more's the pity."

WILLIAM SHAKSPEARE.

" The evening admonition, delivered by him unto the household....."

SIR THOMAS.

" What! and did he indeed shew wind enough for that? Prithee out with it, if thou didst put it into thy tablets."

WILLIAM SHAKSPEARE.

" Alack, sir! there were so many Latin words, I fear me I should be at fault in such attempt."

SIR THOMAS.

" Fear not; we can help thee out between us, were there a dozen or a score."

WILLIAM SHAKSPEARE.

" Bating those latinities, I do verily think I could tie up again most of the points in his doublet."

SIR THOMAS.

" At him then! What was his bearing?"

WILLIAM SHAKSPEARE.

" In dividing his matter, he spooned out and apportioned the commons in his discourse, as best suited the quality, capacity, and constitution of his hearers. To those in priests' orders he delivered a sort of catechism."

SIR SILAS.

" He catechise grown men! He catechise men in priests' orders! being no bishop, nor bishop's ordinary!"

WILLIAM SHAKSPEARE.

" He did so ; it may be at his peril."

SIR THOMAS.

" And what else ? for catechisms are baby's pap."

WILLIAM SHAKSPEARE.

" He did not catechise, but he admonished, the richer gentlemen with gold tassels for their top-knots."

SIR SILAS.

" I thought as much. It was no better in my time. Admonitions fell gently upon those gold tassels; and they ripened degrees as glass and sunshine ripen cucumbers. We priests, forsooth, are catechised! The worst question to any gold tasseller is, ' *How do you do ?*' Old *Alma Mater* coaxes and would be coaxed. But let her look sharp, or spectacles may be thrust upon her nose that shall make her eyes water. Aristotle could make out no royal road to wisdom; but this old woman of ours will shew you one, an you tip her.

" Tilley valley !* catechise priests, indeed !"

* *Tilley valley* was the favourite adjuration of James the Second. It appears in the comedies of Shakspeare.

SIR THOMAS.

" Peradventure he did it discreetly. Let us examine and judge him. Repeat thou what he said unto them."

WILLIAM SHAKSPEARE.

" ' Many,' said he, ' are ingenuous, many are devout, some timidly, some strenuously, but nearly all flinch, and rear, and kick, at the slightest touch, or least inquisitive suspicion of an unsound part in their doctrine. And yet, my brethren, we ought rather to flinch and feel sore at our own searching touch, our own serious inquisition into ourselves. Let us preachers, who are sufficiently liberal in bestowing our advice upon others, inquire of ourselves whether the exercise of spiritual authority may not be sometimes too pleasant, tickling our breasts with a plume from Satan's wing, and turning our heads with that inebriating poison which he hath been seen to instil into the very chalice of our salvation.

Let us ask ourselves in the closet, whether, after we have humbled ourselves before God in our prayers, we never rise beyond the due standard in the pulpit; whether our zeal for the truth be never over-heated by internal fires less holy; whether we never grow stiffly and sternly pertinacious, at the very time when we are reproving the obstinacy of others; and whether we have not frequently so acted as if we believed that opposition were to be relaxed and borne away by self-sufficiency and intolerance. Believe me, the wisest of us have our catechism to learn; and these, my dear friends, are not the only questions contained in it. No Christian can hate; no Christian can malign: nevertheless, do we not often both hate and malign those unhappy men who are insensible to God's mercies? And I fear this unchristian spirit swells darkly, with all its venom, in the marble of our hearts, not because our brother is insensible to these mercies, but because he is insensible to our faculty of persuasion, turning a deaf ear unto our claim upon his obedience, or a blind or sleepy eye upon the fountain of light, whereof we deem ourselves the sacred reservoirs. There is one more question at which ye will tremble when ye ask it in the recesses of your souls: I do tremble at it, yet must utter it. Whether we do not more warmly and erectly stand up for God's word because it came from our mouths, than because it came from his? Learned and ingenious men may indeed find a solution and excuse for all these propositions; but the wise unto salvation will cry, Forgive me, O my God, if, called by thee to walk in thy way, I have not swept this dust from the sanctuary!'"

SIR THOMAS.

" All this, methinks, is for the behoof of clerks and ministers."

WILLIAM SHAKSPEARE.

" He taught them what they who teach

others should learn and practise. Then did he look towards the young gentlemen of large fortune: and lastly his glances fell upon us poorer folk, whom he instructed in the duty we owe to our superiors."

SIR THOMAS.

" Ay, there he had a host."

WILLIAM SHAKSPEARE.

" In one part of his admonition he said,

" ' Young gentlemen ! let not the highest of you who hear me this evening be led into the delusion, for such it is, that the founder of his family was *originally* a greater or a better man than the lowest here. He willed it, and became it. He must have stood low; he must have worked hard; and with tools, moreover, of his own invention and fashioning. He waved and whistled off ten thousand strong and importunate temptations; he dashed the dice-box from the jewelled hand of Chance, the cup from Pleasure's, and trod under foot the sorceries of each; he ascended steadily the precipices of Danger, and looked down with intrepidity from the summit; he overawed arrogance with sedateness; he seized by the horn and overleaped low Violence; and he fairly swung Fortune round.

" 'The very high cannot rise much higher; the very low may: the truly great must have done it.

" ' This is not the doctrine, my friends, of the silkenly and lawnly religious; it wears the coarse texture of the fisherman, and walks uprightly and straightforward under it. I am speaking now more particularly to you amongst us upon whom God hath laid the incumbrances of wealth, the sweets whereof bring teazing and poisonous things about you, not easily sent away. What now are your pretensions under sacks of money? or your enjoyments under the shade of genealogical trees? Are they rational? Are they real? Do they exist at all? Strange inconsistency! to be proud of having as much gold and silver laid upon yon as a mule hath, and yet to carry it less composedly! The mule is not answerable for the conveyance and discharge of his burden : you are. Stranger infatuation still! to be prouder of an excellent thing done by another than by yourselves, supposing any excellent thing to have actually been done ; and, after all, to be more elated on his cruelties than his kindnesses, by the blood he hath spilt than by the benefits he hath conferred ; and to acknowledge less obligation to a well-informed and well-intentioned progenitor than to a lawless and ferocious barbarian. Would stocks and stumps, if they could ntter words, utter such gross stupidity? Would the apple boast of his crab origin, or the peach of his prune? Hardly any man is ashamed of being inferior to his ancestors, although it is the very thing at which the great should blush, if, indeed, the great in general descended from the worthy.

I did expect to see the day, and although I shall not see it, it must come at last, when he shall be treated as a madman or an impostor who dares to claim nobility or precedency, and cannot shew his family name in the history of his country.   Even he who can shew it, and who cannot write his own under it in the same or as goodly characters, must submit to the imputation of degeneracy, from which the lowly and obscure are exempt.

" ' He alone who maketh you wiser, maketh you greater; and it is only by such an implement that Almighty God himself effects it. When he taketh away a man's wisdom, he taketh away his strength, his power over others and over himself.   What help for him, then! He may sit idly and swell his spleen, saying — *Who is this? who is that?* and at the question's end the spirit of inquiry dies away in him.   It would not have been so, if, in happier hour, he had said within himself— *Who am I?*

what am I? and had prosecuted the search in good earnest.

" ' When we ask who *this* man is, or who *that* man is, we do not expect or hope for a plain answer : we should be disappointed at a direct, or a rational, or a kind one. We desire to hear that he was of low origin, or had committed some crime, or been subjected to some calamity. Whoever he be, in general we disregard or despise him, unless we discover that he possesseth by nature many qualities of mind and body which he never brings into use, and many accessories of situation and fortune which he brings into abuse every day. According to the arithmetic in practice, he who makes the most idlers and the most in-grates is the most worshipful. But wiser ones than the scorers in this school will tell you how riches and power were bestowed by Pro-vidence, that generosity and mercy should be exercised : for, if every gift of the Almighty were distributed in equal portions to every creature, less of such virtues would be called into the field; consequently there would be less of gratitude, less of submission, less of devotion, less of hope, and, in the total, less of content.'"

Here he ceased, and Sir Thomas nodded, and said—

" Reasonable enough! nay, almost too reasonable !

" But where are the apostles? Where are the disciples? Where are the saints? Where is hell-fire?

" Well! patience! we may come to it yet. Go on, Will !"

With such encouragement before him, did Will Shakspeare take breath and continue :

" ' We mortals are too much accustomed to behold our superiors in rank and station as we behold the leaves in the forest. While we stand under these leaves, our protection and refuge from heat and labour, we see only the rougher side of them, and the gloominess of the branches on which they hang. In the midst of their benefits we are insensible to their utility and their beauty, and appear to be ignorant that, if they were placed less high above us, we should derive from them less advantage.'"

SIR THOMAS.

" Ay; envy of superiority made the angels kick and run restive."

WILLIAM SHAKSPEARE.

" May it please your worship! with all my faults, I have ever borne submission and reverence toward my superiors."

SIR THOMAS.

" Very right! very scriptural! But most folks do that. Our duty is not fulfilled unless we bear absolute veneration; unless we are ready to lay down our lives and fortunes at the foot of the throne, and every thing else at the foot of those who administer the laws under virgin majesty."

WILLIAM SHAKSPEARE.

" Honoured sir! I am quite ready to lay down my life and fortune, and all the rest of me, before that great virgin."

SIR SILAS.

" Thy life and fortune, to wit!

" What are they worth? A June cob-nut, maggot and all."

SIR THOMAS.

" Silas! we will not repudiate nor rebuff this Magdalen, that bringeth a pot of ointment. Rather let us teach and tutor than twit. It is a tractable and conducible youth, being in good company."

SIR SILAS.

" Teach and tutor! Hold hard, sir! These base varlets ought to be taught but two thiugs: to bow as beseemeth them to their betters, and to hang perpendicular. We have authority for it, that no man can add an inch to his stature, but, by aid of the sheriff, I engage to find a chap who shall add two or three to this whoreson's." *

SIR THOMAS.

" Nay, nay, now, Silas! the lad's mother was always held to be an honest woman."

SIR SILAS.

" His mother may be an honest woman for me."

WILLIAM SHAKSPEARE.

" No small privilege, by my faith! for any woman in the next parish to thee, Master Silas!"

SIR SILAS.

" There again! out comes the filthy runlet

---

* *Whoreson,* if we may hazard a conjecture, means the son of a woman of ill-repute. In this we are borne out by the context. It appears to have escaped the commentators on Shakspeare.

Whoreson, a word of frequent occurrence in the comedies; more rarely found in the tragedies. Although now obsolete, the expression proves that there were (or were believed to be) such persons formerly.

The Editor is indebted to two learned friends for these two remarks, which appear no less just than ingenious.

from the quagmire, that but now lay so quiet with all its own in it."

WILLIAM SHAKSPEARE.

" Until it was trodden on by the ass that could not leap over it.   These, I think, are the words of the fable."

SIR THOMAS.

" They are so."

SIR SILAS.

" What fable ?"

SIR THOMAS.

" Tush ! don't press him too hard : he wants not wit, but learning."

SIR SILAS.

" He wants a rope's-end ; and a rope's-end is not enough for him, unless we throw in the other."

SIR THOMAS.

" Peradventure he may be an instrument, a potter's clay, a type, a token.

" I have seen many young men, and none

like unto him.   He is shallow but clear; he is simple, but ingenuous."

SIR SILAS.

" Drag the ford again, then.   In my mind he is as deep as the big tankard; and a mouthful of rough beverage will be the beginning and end of it."

SIR THOMAS.

" No fear of that.   Neither, if rightly reported by the youngster, is there so much doctrine in the doctor as we expected.   He doth not dwell upon the main; he is worldly; he is wise in his generation; he says things out of his own head.

" Silas, that can't hold! We want *props— fulcrums*, I think you called 'em, to the farmers; or was it *stimulums ?*"

SIR SILAS.

" Both very good words."

SIR THOMAS.

" I should be mightily pleased to hear thee dispute with that great don."

SIR SILAS.

" I hate disputations. Saint Paul warns us against them. If one wants to be thirsty, the tail of a stockfish is as good for it as the head of a logician.

" The doctor there, at Oxford, is in flesh and mettle : but let him be sleek and gingered as he may, clap me in Saint Mary's pulpit, cassock me, lamb-skin me, give me pink for my colours, glove me to the elbow, heel-piece me half an ell high, cushion me before and behind, bring me a mug of mild ale and a rasher of bacon, only just to con over the text withal ; then allow me fair play, and as much of my own way as he had, and the devil take the hindermost. I am his man at any time."

SIR THOMAS.

" I am fain to believe it. Verily, I do think, Silas, thou hast as much stuff in thee as most men. Our beef and mutton at Charlecote rear other than babes and sucklings.

" I like words taken, like thine, from black-letter books. They look stiff and sterling, and as though a man might dig about 'em for a week, and never loosen the lightest.

" Thou hast alway at hand either saint or devil, as occasion needeth, according to the quality of the sinner, and they never come uncalled for. Moreover, Master Silas, I have observed that thy hell-fire is generally lighted up in the pulpit about the dog-days."

Then turned the worthy knight unto the youth, saying,

" 'Twere well for thee, William Shakspeare, if the learned doctor had kept thee longer in his house, and had shewn unto thee the danger of idleness, which hath often led unto deer-stealing and poetry. In thee we already know the one, although the distemper hath eaten but skin-deep for the present; and we have the testimony of two burgesses on the other. The pursuit of poetry, as likewise of game, is unforbidden to persons of condition."

WILLIAM SHAKSPEARE.

" Sir, that of game is the more likely to keep them in it."

SIR THOMAS.

" It is the more knightly of the two; but poetry hath also her pursuers among us. I myself, in my youth, had some experience that way; and I am fain to blush at the reputation I obtained. His honour, my father, took me to London at the age of twenty; and, sparing no expense in my education, gave fifty shillings to one Monsieur Dubois to teach me fencing and poetry, in twenty lessons. In vacant hours he taught us also the laws of honour, which are different from ours.

" In France you are unpolite, unless you solicit a judge or his wife to favour your cause, and you inevitably lose it. In France there is no want of honour where there is no want of courage: you may lie, but you must not hear that you lie. I asked him what he thought then of lying; and he replied,

" ' *C'est selon.*'

" And suppose you should overhear the whisper?

" ' *Ah parbleu! Cela m'irrite; cela me pousse au bout.*'

" I was going on to remark that a real man of honour could less bear to lie than to hear it; when he cried, at the words *real man of honour,*

" ' *Le voilà, Monsieur! le voilà!*' and gave himself such a blow on the breast as convinced me the French are a brave people.

" He told us that nothing but his honour was left him, but that it supplied the place of all he had lost. It was discovered some time afterwards that M. Dubois had been guilty of perjury, had been a spy, and had lost nothing but a dozen or two of tin patty-pans, hereditary in his family, his father having been a cook on his own account.

" William, it is well at thy time of life that thou shouldst know the customs of far

countries, particularly if it should be the will
of God to place thee in a company of players.
Of all nations in the world, the French best
understand the stage. If thou shouldst ever
write for it, which God forbid, copy them very
carefully. Murders on their stage are quite
decorous and cleanly. For gentlemen and
ladies die by violence who would not have
died by exhaustion. 'For they rant and rave
until their voice fails them, one after another;
and those who do not die of it, die consumptive.
These cannot bear to see cruelty: they would
rather see any image than their own.' These
are not my observations, but were made by
Sir Everard Starkeye, who likewise did remark to Monsieur Dubois, that ' cats, if you
hold them up to the looking-glass, will scratch
you terribly; and that the same fierce animal,
as if proud of its cleanly coat and its velvety
paw, doth carefully put aside what other
animals of more estimation take no trouble
to conceal.'

I

"'Our people,' said Sir Everard, 'must see upon the stage what they never could have imagined; so the best men in the world would earnestly take a peep of hell through a chink, whereas the worser would skulk away.'

"Do not thou be their caterer William! Avoid the writing of comedies and tragedies. To make people laugh is uncivil, and to make people cry is unkind. And what, after all, are these comedies and these tragedies? They are what, for the benefit of all future generations, I have myself described them,

> 'The whimsies of wantons and stories of dread,
>   That make the stout-hearted look under the bed.'

Furthermore, let me warn thee against the same on account of the vast charges thou must stand at. We Englishmen cannot find it in our hearts to murder a man without much difficulty, hesitation, and delay. We have little or no invention for pains and penalties; it is only our acutest lawyers who have wit enough to frame them. Therefore it behoveth your tragedy-man to provide a rich assortment of them, in order to strike the auditor with awe and wonder. And a tragedy-man, in our country, who cannot afford a fair dozen of stabbed males, and a trifle under that mask of poisoned females, and chains enow to moor a whole navy in dock, is but a scurvy fellow at the best. Thou wilt find trouble in purveying these necessaries; and then must come the gim-cracks for the second course; gods, goddesses, fates, furies, battles, marriages, music, and the maypole. Hast thou within thee wherewithal?"

" Sir!" replied Billy, with great modesty, " I am most grateful for these ripe fruits of your experience. To admit delightful visions into my own twilight chamber, is not dangerous nor forbidden. Believe me, sir, he who indulges in them will abstain from injuring his neighbour: he will see no glory in peril, and no delight in strife.

" The world shall never be troubled by any

battles and marriages of mine, and I desire no other music and no other maypole than have lightened my heart at Stratford."

Sir Thomas finding him well-conditioned and manageable, proceeded:

" Although I have admonished thee of sundry and insurmountable impediments, yet more are lying in the pathway. We have no verse for tragedy. One in his hurry hath dropped rhyme, and walketh like unto the man who wanteth the left-leg stocking. Others can give us rhyme indeed, but can hold no longer after the tenth or eleventh syllable. Now Sir Everard Starkeye, who is a pretty poet, did confess to Monsieur Dubois the potency of the French tragic verse, which thou never canst hope to bring over.

" ' I wonder, Monsieur Dubois !' said Sir Everard, ' that your countrymen should have thought it necessary to transport their heavy artillery into Italy. No Italian could stand a volley of your heroic verses from the best and biggest pieces.   With these brought into action, you never could have lost the battle of Pavia.'

" Now my friend Sir Everard is not quite so good a historian as he is a poet: and Monsieur Dubois took advantage of him.

" ' Pardon! Monsieur Sir Everard!' said Monsieur Dubois, smiling at my friend's slip, ' we did not lose the battle of Pavia.   We had the misfortune to lose our king, who delivered himself up, as our kings always do, for the good and glory of his country.'

" ' How was this?' said Sir Everard, in surprise.

" ' I will tell you, Monsieur Sir Everard!' said Monsieur Dubois.   ' I had it from my own father, who fought in the battle, and told my mother, word for word:

" ' The king seeing his household troops, being only one thousand strong, surrounded by twelve regiments, the best Spanish troops, amounting to eighteen thousand four hundred and forty-two, although he doubted not of victory, yet thought he might lose many brave men before the close of the day, and rode up instantly to King Charles, and said,

" ' My brother! I am loath to lose so many of those brave men yonder. Whistle off your Spanish pointers, and I agree to ride home with you.'

" ' And so he did.   But what did King Charles? abusing French loyalty, he made our Francis his prisoner, would you believe it? and treated him worse than ever badger was treated at the bottom of any paltry stable-yard, putting upon his table beer and Rhenish wine and wild boar.'

" I have digressed with thee, young man," continued the knight, much to the improvement of my knowledge, I do reverentially confess, as it was of the lad's. " We will now," said he, " endeavour our best to sober thee, finding that Doctor Glaston hath omitted it."

" Not entirely omitted it," said William, gratefully ; " he did towards it, after dinner, all that could be done at such a time towards it. The doctor could, however, speak only of the Greeks and Romans, and certainly what he said of them gave me but little encouragement."

SIR THOMAS.

" What said he ?"

WILLIAM SHAKSPEARE.

" He said, ' the Greeks conveyed all their wisdom into their theatre; their stages were churches and parliament-houses; but what was false prevailed over what was true. They had their own wisdom; the wisdom of the foolish. Who is Sophocles, if compared to Doctor Hammersley of Oriel? or Euripides, if compared to Doctor Prichard of Jesus? Without the Gospel, light is darkness; and with it, children are giants.

" ' William, I need not expatiate on Greek with thee, since thou knowest it not, but some crumbs of Latin are picked up by the callowest beaks. The Romans had, as thou findest, and have still, more taste for murder than morality, and, as they could not find heroes among them, looked for gladiators. Their only very high poet employed his elevation and strength to dethrone and debase the Deity. They had several others, who polished their language and pitched their instruments with admirable skill: several who glared over their thin and flimsy gaberdines many bright feathers from the wide-spread downs of Ionia, and the richly cultivated rocks of Attica.

" ' Some of them have spoken from inspiration: for thou art not to suppose that from the heathen were withheld all the manifestations of the Lord. We do agree at Oxford that the Pollio of Virgil is our Saviour. True, it is the dullest and poorest poem that a nation not very poetical has bequeathed unto us; and even the versification, in which this master excelled, is wanting in fluency and sweetness. I can only account for this from the weight of the subject. Two verses, which are fairly worth two hundred such poems, are from another pagan : he was forced to sigh for the church without knowing her : he saith,

> ' May I gaze upon thee when my latest hour is come!
> May I hold thy hand when mine faileth me !'

This, if adumbrating the church, is the most beautiful thought that ever issued from the heart of man : but if addressed to a wanton, as some do opine, is filth from the sink, nauseating and insufferable.

" ' William ! that which moveth the heart most is the best poetry; it comes nearest unto God, the source of all power.' "

SIR THOMAS.

" ' Yea; and he appeareth unto me to know more of poetry than of divinity. Those ancients have little flesh upon the body poetical, and lack the savour that sufficeth. The Song of Solomon drowns all their voices : they seem but whistlers and guitar-players compared to a full-cheeked trumpeter; they standing under the eaves in some dark lane, he upon a wellcaparisoned stallion, tossing his mane and all his ribands to the sun. I doubt the doctor spake too fondly of the Greeks; they were giddy creatures. William! I am loath to be hard on them ; but they please me not. There are those now living who could make them bite their nails to the quick, and turn green as grass with envy."

WILLIAM SHAKSPEARE.

" Sir, one of those Greeks, methinks, thrown into the pickle-pot, would be a treasure to the housewife's young jerkins."

SIR THOMAS.

" Simpleton! simpleton! but thou valuest them justly.—Now attend. If ever thou shouldst hear, at Oxford or London, the verses I am about to repeat, prythee do not communicate them to that fiery spirit Mat Atterend. It might not be the battle of two hundreds, but two counties; a sort of York and Lancaster war, whereof I would wash my hands. Listen !"

And now did Sir Thomas clear his voice, always high and sonorous, and did repeat from the stores of his memory these rich and proud verses.

" ' Chloe! mean men must ever make mean loves,
They deal in dog-roses, but I in cloves.
They are just scorch'd enough to blow their fingers,
I am a phœnix downright burnt to cinders.' "

At which noble conceits, so far above what poor Bill had ever imagined, he lifted up his eyes to heaven, and exclaimed,

" The world itself must be reduced to that condition before such glorious verses die! *Chloe* and *Clove*! Why, sir! Chloe wants but a V towards the tail to become the very thing! Never tell me that such matters can come about of themselves. And how truly is it said that we mean men deal in dog-roses!

" Sir, if it were permitted me to swear on that holy Bible, I would swear I never until this day heard that dog-roses were our provender; and yet did I, no longer ago than last summer,

write, not indeed upon a dog-rose, but upon a
sweet-briar, what would only serve to rince
the mouth withal after the clove."

SIR THOMAS.

" Repeat the same, youth! We may haply
give thee our counsel thereupon."

Willy took heart, and, lowering his voice,
which hath much natural mellowness, repeated
these from memory :

> " My briar that smelledst sweet
>   When gentle spring's first heat
>   Ran through thy quiet veins;
>   Thou that couldst injure none,
>   But wouldst be left alone,
> Alone thou leavest me, and nought of thine remains.

> " What ! hath no poet's lyre
>   O'er thee, sweet-breathing briar,
>   Hung fondly, ill or well?
>   And yet methinks with thee
>   A poet's sympathy,
> Whether in weal or woe, in life or death, might dwell.

> " Hard usage both must bear,
>   Few hands your youth will rear,
>   Few bosoms cherish you ;

> Your tender prime must bleed
> Ere you are sweet, but freed
> From life, you then are prized; thus prized are poets too."

Sir Thomas said, with kind encouragement, "He who beginneth so discreetly with a dog-rose, may hope to encompass a damask-rose ere he die."

Willy did now breathe freely. The commendation of a knight and magistrate worked powerfully within him: and Sir Thomas said furthermore,

"These short matters do not suit me. Thou mightest have added some moral about life and beauty: poets never handle roses without one; but thou art young, and mayest get into the train."

Willy made the best excuse he could; and no bad one it was, the knight acknowledged; namely, that the sweet-briar was not really dead although left for dead.

"Then," said Sir Thomas, " as life and beauty would not serve thy turn, thou mightest have had full enjoyment of the beggar, the wayside, the thieves, and the good Samaritan,— enough to tapestry the bridal chamber of an empress."

William bowed respectfully, and sighed.

" Ha ! thou hast lost them, sure enough, and it may not be quite so fair to smile at thy quandary," quoth Sir Thomas.

" I did my best the first time," said Willy, " and fell short the second."

" That indeed thou must have done," said Sir Thomas. " It is a grievous disappointment, in the midst of our lamentations for the dead, to find ourselves balked. I am curious to see how thou couldst help thyself. Don't be abashed ; I am ready for even worse than the last."

Bill hesitated, but obeyed :

> " And art thou yet alive ?
> And shall the happy hive
>   Send out her youth to cull
> Thy sweets of leaf and flower,

> And spend the sunny hour
> With thee, and thy faint heart with murmuring music lull?
>
> " Tell me what tender care,
> Tell me what pious prayer,
> Bade thee arise and live?
> The fondest-favoured bee
> Shall whisper nought to thee
> More loving than the song my grateful muse shall give."

Sir Thomas looked somewhat less pleased at the conclusion of these verses than at the conclusion of the former; and said gravely,

" Young man! methinks it is betimes that thou talkest of having a muse to thyself; or even in common with others. It is only great poets who have muses; I mean to say, who have the right to talk in that fashion. The French, I hear, *Phœbus* it and *muse-me* it right and left; and boggle not to throw all nine, together with mother and master, into the compass of a dozen lines or thereabout. And your Italian can hardly do without 'em in the multiplication-table. We Englishmen do let them in quietly, shut the door, and say nothing of what passes.   I have read a whole book of comedies, and ne'er a muse to help the lamest."

WILLIAM SHAKSPEARE.

" Wonderful forbearance!   I marvel how the poet could get through."

SIR THOMAS.

" By God's help.   And I think we did as well without 'em : for it must be an unabashable man that ever shook his sides in their company.   They lay heavy restraint both upon laughing and crying.   In the great master Virgil of Rome, they tell me they come in to count the ships, and having cast up the sum total, and proved it, make off again.   Sure token of two things : first, that he held 'em dog-cheap ; secondly, that he had made but little progress (for a Lombard born) in book-keeping in double entry.

" He, and every other great genius, began with small subject-matters, gnats and the like. I myself, similar unto him, wrote upon fruit. I would give thee some copies for thy copying, if I thought thou wouldst use them temperately, and not render them common, as hath befallen the poetry of some among the brightest geniuses. I could shew thee how to say new things, and how to time the same. Before my day, nearly all the flowers and fruits had been gathered by poets, old and young, *from the cedar of Lebanon to the hyssop on the wall:* roses went up to Solomon, apples to Adam, and so forth.

" Willy! my brave lad! I was the firs that ever handled a quince, I'll be sworn.

" Hearken!

" Chloe! I would not have thee wince,
   That I unto thee send a quince.
   I would not have thee say unto't
   Begone! and trample't underfoot,
   For, trust me, 'tis no fulsome fruit.
   It came not out of mine own garden,
   But all the way from Henly in Arden,—
   Of an uncommon fine old tree,
   Belonging to John Apsbury.
   And if that of it thou shalt eat,
   'Twill make thy breath e'en yet more sweet;

> As a translation here doth shew,
> *On fruit-trees, by Jean Mirabeau.*
> The frontispiece is printed so.
> But eat it with some wine and cake,
> Or it may give the belly-ake.*
> This doth my worthy clerk indite,
> I sign,
> > SIR THOMAS LUCY, Knight."

" Now, Willy, there is not one poet or lover in twenty who careth for consequences. Many hint to the lady what to do; few what not to do; although it would oftentimes, as in this case, go to one's heart to see the upshot."

" Ah, sir!" said Bill, in all humility, " I would make bold to put the parings of that quince under my pillow, for sweet dreams and insights, if Doctor Glaston had given me encouragement to continue the pursuit of

---

* *Belly-ake,* more properly spelt *belly-ache,* a disorder once not uncommon in England. Even the name is now almost forgotten; yet the elder of us may remember at least the report of it, and some, perhaps, even the complaint itself, in our schooldays. It usually broke out about the cherry season; and, in some cases, made its appearance again at the first nutting.

poetry. Of a surety it would bless me with a bedful of churches and crucifixions, duly adumbrated."

Whereat Sir Thomas, shaking his head, did inform him,

" It was in the golden age of the world, as pagans call it, that poets of condition sent fruits and flowers to their beloved, with posies fairly penned. We, in our days, have done the like. But manners of late are much corrupted on the one side, if not on both.

" Willy! it hath been whispered that there be those who would rather have a piece of brocade or velvet for a stomacher, than the touchingest copy of verses, with a bleeding heart at the bottom."

WILLIAM SHAKSPEARE.

" Incredible!"

SIR THOMAS.

" 'Tis even so!"

WILLIAM SHAKSPEARE.

" They must surely be rotten fragments

of the world before the flood,— saved out of it by the devil."

SIR THOMAS.

" I am not of that mind.

" Their eyes, mayhap, fell upon some of the bravery cast ashore from the Spanish Armada.   In ancienter days, a few pages of good poetry outvalued a whole ell of the finest Genoa."

WILLIAM SHAKSPEARE.

" When will such days return !"

SIR THOMAS.

" It is only within these few years that corruption and avarice have made such ghastly strides.   They always did exist, but were gentler.

" My youth is waning, and has been nigh upon these seven years, I being now in my forty-eighth."

WILLIAM SHAKSPEARE.

" I have understood that the god of poetry

is in the enjoyment of eternal youth; I was
ignorant that his sons were."

SIR THOMAS.

" No, child! we are hale and comely,
but must go the way of all flesh."

WILLIAM SHAKSPEARE.

" Must it, can it, be ?"

SIR THOMAS.

" Time was, my smallest gifts were accept-
able, as thus recorded : —

> " From my fair hand, O will ye, will ye
>   Deign humbly to accept a gilly-
>   Flower for thy bosom, sugared maid !
>
> " Scarce had I said it, ere she took it,
>   And in a twinkling, faith ! had stuck it,
>   Where e'en proud knighthood might have laid."

William was now quite unable to contain
himself, and seemed utterly to have forgotten
the grievous charge against him; to such a
pitch did his joy o'erleap his jeopardy.

Master Silas in the meantime was much
disquieted; and first did he strip away all

the white feather from every pen in the ink-
pot, and then did he mend them, one and all,
and then did he slit them with his thumb-
nail, and then did he pare and slash away
at them again, and then did he cut off the
tops, until at last he left upon them neither
nib nor plume, nor enough of the middle
to serve as quill to a virginal. It went to
my heart to see such a power of pens so
wasted : there could not be fewer than five.
Sir Thomas was less wary than usual, being
overjoyed. For great poets do mightily affect
to have little poets under them; and little
poets do forget themselves in great company,
as fiddlers do, who *hail fellow well met!* even
with lords.

Sir Thomas did not interrupt our Bill's
wild gladness. I never thought so worshipful
a personage could bear so much. At last he
said unto the lad :

" I do bethink me, if thou hearest much
more of my poetry, and the success attendant

thereon, good Doctor Glaston would tear thy skirt off, ere he could drag thee back from the occupation."

WILLIAM SHAKSPEARE.

" I fear me, for once, all his wisdom would sluice out in vain."

SIR THOMAS.

" It was reported to me, that when our virgin queen's highness (her Dear Dread's* ear not being then poisoned) heard these verses, she said before her courtiers, to the sore travail of some, and heart's content of others,—

" ' We need not envy our young cousin James of Scotland his ass's bite of a thistle, having such flowers as these gilliflowers on the chimney-stacks of Charlecote.'

" I could have told her highness that all this poetry, from beginning to end, was real matter of fact, well and truly spoken by mine

* Sir Thomas borrowed this expression from Spenser, who thus calls Queen Elizabeth.

own self. I had only to harness the rhymes thereunto, at my leisure."

WILLIAM SHAKSPEARE.

" None could ever doubt it. Greeks and Trojans may fight for the quince ; neither shall have it

> While a Warwickshire lad
> Is on earth to be had,
> With a wand to wag
> On a trusty nag,
> He shall keep the lists
> With cudgel or fists.
> And black shall be whose eye
> Looks evil on Lucy."

SIR THOMAS.

" Nay, nay, nay! do not trespass too soon upon heroics. Thou seest thou canst not hold thy wind beyond eight lines. What wouldst thou do under the heavy mettle that should have wrought such wonders at Pavia, if thou findest these petards so troublesome in discharging? Surely, the good doctor, had he entered at large on the subject, would have been very particular in urging this expostulation."

WILLIAM SHAKSPEARE.

" Sir, to my mortification I must confess, that I took to myself the counsel he was giving to another; a young gentleman who, from his pale face, his abstinence at table, his cough, his taciturnity, and his gentleness, seemed already more than half poet. To him did Doctor Glaston urge, with all his zeal and judgment, many arguments against the vocation; telling him that, even in college, he had few applauders, being the first, and not the second or third, who always are more fortunate; reminding him that he must solicit and obtain much interest with men of rank and quality, before he could expect their favour; and that without it the vein chilled, the nerve relaxed, and the poet was left at next door to the bellman. ' In the coldness of the world,' said he, ' in the absence of ready friends and adherents, to light thee upstairs to the richly tapestried chamber of the muses, thy spirits will abandon thee, thy heart will sicken and swell within thee; overladen, thou wilt make, O Ethelbert! a slow and painful progress, and, ere the door open, sink. Praise giveth weight unto the wanting, and happiness giveth elasticity unto the heavy. As the mightier streams of the unexplored world, America, run languidly in the night,* and await the sun on high to contend with him in strength and grandeur, so doth genius halt and pause in the thraldom of outspread darkness, and move onward with all his vigour then only when creative light and jubilant warmth surround him.'

" Ethelbert coughed faintly; a tinge of red, the size of a rose-bud, coloured the middle of his cheek; and yet he seemed not to be pained by the reproof. He looked fondly and affectionately at his teacher, who thus proceeded:

" ' My dear youth, do not carry the stone

---

* Humboldt notices this.

of Sisyphus on thy shoulder to pave the way to disappointment. If thou writest but indifferent poetry, none will envy thee and some will praise thee: but nature, in her malignity, hath denied unto thee a capacity for the enjoyment of such praise. In this she hath been kinder to most others than to thee: we know wherein she hath been kinder to thee than to most others. If thou writest good poetry, many will call it flat, many will call it obscure, many will call it inharmonious; and some of these will speak as they think; for, as in giving a feast to great numbers, it is easier to possess the wine than to procure the cups, so happens it in poetry; thou hast the beverage of thy own growth, but canst not find the recipients. What is simple and elegant to thee and me, to many an honest man is flat and sterile; what to us is an innocently sly allusion, to as worthy a one as either of us is dull obscurity; and that moreover which swims upon our brain, and which throbs against our temples, and which we delight in sounding to ourselves when the voice has done with it, touches their ear, and awakens no harmony in any cell of it. Rivals will run up to thee and call thee a plagiary, and, rather than that proof should be wanting, similar words to some of thine will be thrown in thy teeth out of Leviticus and Deuteronomy.

" ' Do you desire calm studies? Do you desire high thoughts? Penetrate into theology. What is nobler than to dissect and discern the opinions of the gravest men upon the subtilest matters? And what glorious victories are those over Infidelity and Scepticism? How much loftier, how much more lasting in their effects, than such as ye are invited unto by what this ingenious youth hath contemptuously and truly called

" The swaggering drum, and trumpet hoarse with rage."

And what a delightful and edifying sight it is, to see hundreds of the most able doctors, all stripped for the combat, each closing with his antagonist, and tugging and tearing, tooth and nail, to lay down and establish truths which have been floating in the air for ages, and which the lower order of mortals are forbidden to see, and commanded to embrace. And then the shouts of victory! And then the crowns of amaranth held over their heads by the applauding angels. Besides, these combats have other great and distinct advantages. Whereas, in the carnal, the longer ye contend the more blows do ye receive; in these against Satan, the more fiercely and pertinaciously ye drive at him, the slacker do ye find him: every good hit makes him redden and rave with anger, but diminishes its effect.

" ' My dear friends! who would not enter a service in which he may give blows to his mortal enemy, and receive none; and in which not only the eternal gain is incalculable, but also the temporal, at four-and-twenty, may be far above the emolument of generals, who,

before the priest was born, had bled profusely
for his country, established her security, bright-
ened her glory, and augmented her dominions.'"

At this pause did Sir Thomas turn unto
Sir Silas, and asked,

" What sayest thou, Silas?"

Whereupon did Sir Silas make answer—

" I say it is so, and was so, and should be
so, and shall be so.   If the queen's brother had
not sopped the priests and bishops out of the
Catholic cup, they could have held the Catholic cup in their own hands, instead of yielding
it into his.   They earned their money: if they
sold their consciences for it, the business is
theirs, not ours.   I call this facing the devil
with a vengeance.   We have their coats; no
matter who made 'em; we have 'em, I say,
and we will wear 'em; and not a button,
tag, or tassel, shall any man tear away."

Sir Thomas then turned to Willy, and re-
quested him to proceed with the doctor's discourse, who thereupon continued.

" Within your own recollections, how many good, quiet, inoffensive men, unendowed with any extraordinary abilities, have been enabled, by means of divinity, to enjoy a long life in tranquillity and affluence.'

" Whereupon did one of the young gentlemen smile, and, on small encouragement from Doctor Glaston to enounce the cause thereof, he repeated these verses, which he gave afterwards unto me.

" In the names on our books
Was standing Tom Flooke's,
Who took in due time his degrees;
Which when he had taken,
Like an Ascham or Bacon,
By night he could snore, and by day he could sneeze.

" Calm, pithy, pragmatical,*
Tom Flooke he could at a call
Rise up like a hound from his sleep;
And if many a quarto
He gave not his heart to,
If pellucid in lore, in his cups he was deep.

* *Pragmatical* here means only *precise*.

" He never did harm,
   And his heart might be warm,
For his doublet most certainly was so;
   And now has Tom Flooke
   A quieter nook
Than ever had Spenser or Tasso.

" He lives in his house,
   As still as a mouse,
Until he has eaten his dinner;
   But then doth his nose
   Outroar all the woes
That encompass the death of a sinner.

" And there oft has been seen
   No less than a dean
To tarry a week in the parish,
   In October and March,
   When deans are less starch,
And days are less gleamy and garish.

" That Sunday Tom's eyes
   Look'd always more wise,
He repeated more often his text;
   Two leaves stuck together,
   (The fault of the weather)
And....*the rest ye shall hear in my next.*

" At mess he lost quite
   His small appetite,
By losing his friend the good dean:

> The cook's sight must fail her!
> The eggs sure are staler!
> The beef too!   Why, what can it mean?
>   " He turned off the butcher,
>   To the cook, could he clutch her,
> What his choler had done there's no saying ..
>   'Tis verily said
>   He smote low the cock's head,
> And took other pullets for laying."

" On this being concluded, Doctor Glaston said he shrewdly suspected an indigestion on the part of Mr. Thomas Flooke, caused by sitting up late and studying hard with Mr. Dean ; and protested that theology itself should not carry us into the rawness of the morning air, particularly in such critical months as March and October, in one of which the sap rises, in the other sinks, and there are many stars very sinister."

Sir Thomas shook his head, and declared he would not be uncharitable to rector, or dean, or doctor, but that certain surmises swam uppermost.   He then winked at Master Silas, who said, incontinently,

"You have it, Sir Thomas! The blind buzzards! with their stars and saps!"

"Well, but Silas! you yourself have told us over and over again, in church, that there are *arcana*."

"So there are; I uphold it," replied Master Silas, "but a fig for the greater part, and a fig-leaf for the rest! As for these signs, they are as plain as any page in the Revelations."

Sir Thomas, after short pondering, said scoffingly,

"In regard to the rawness of the air having any effect whatsoever on those who discourse orthodoxically on theology, it is quite as absurd as to imagine that a man ever caught cold in a Protestant church. I am rather of opinion that it was a judgment on the rector for his evilmindedness towards the cook, the Lord foreknowing that he was about to be wilful and vengeful in that quarter. It was, however, more advisedly that he took other pullets, on his own view of the case, although it might be that the same pullets would suit him again as well as ever, when his appetite should return; for it doth not appear that they were loath to lay, but laid somewhat unsatisfactorily.

" Now, youth!" continued his worship, " if in our clemency we should spare thy life, study this higher elegiacal strain which thou hast carried with thee from Oxford: it containeth, over and above an unusual store of biography, much sound moral doctrine, for those who are heedful in the weighing of it. And what can be more affecting than,

> ' At mess he lost quite
> His small appetite,
> By losing his friend the good dean!'

And what an insight into character! Store it up; store it up! *Small appetite*, particular; *good dean*, generick."

" Hereupon did Master Silas jerk me with his indicative joint, the elbow to wit, and did say in my ear,

" He means *deanery*. Give me one of those bones so full of marrow, and let my lord bishop have all the meat over it, and welcome. If a dean is not on his stilts, he is not on his stumps: he stands on his own ground: he is a *noli-me-tangeretarian*."

" What art thou saying of those sectaries, good Master Silas!" quoth Sir Thomas, not hearing him distinctly.

" I was talking of the dean," replied Master Silas. " He was the very dean who wrote and sang that song called the *Two Jacks*."

" Hast it?" asked he.

Master Silas shook his head, and, trying in vain to recollect it, said at last,

" After dinner it sometimes pops out of a filbert-shell in a crack; and I have known it float on the first glass of Herefordshire cider; it also hath some affinity with very stiff and old bottled beer; but in a morning it seemeth unto me like a remnant of over-night "

" Our memory waneth, Master Silas !"
quoth Sir Thomas, looking seriously. " If thou
couldst repeat it, without the grimace of singing, it were not ill."

Master Silas struck the table with his fist,
and repeated the first stave angrily; but in
the second he forgot the admonition of Sir
Thomas, and did sing outright,

> " Jack Calvin and Jack Cade,
>   Two gentles of one trade,
>   Two tinkers,
>   Very gladly would pull down
>   Mother Church and Father Crown,
>   And would starve or would drown
>   Right thinkers.

> " Honest man ! honest man !
>   Fill the can, fill the can,
> They are coming ! they are coming ! they are coming !
>   If any drop be left,
>   It might tempt 'em to a theft....
> Zooks ! it was only the ale that was humming."

" In the first stave, gramercy ! there is an
awful verity," quoth Sir Thomas; " but I

wonder that a dean should let his skewer slip out, and his fat catch fire so wofully, in the second. Light stuff, Silas! fit only for ale-houses."

Master Silas was nettled in the nose, and answered,

" Let me see the man in Warwickshire, and in all the counties round, who can run at such a rate with so light a feather in the palm of his hand. I am no poet, thank God! but I know what folks can do, and what folks cannot do."

" Well, Silas!" replied Sir Thomas, " after thy thanksgiving for being no poet, let us have the rest of the piece."

" The rest!" quoth Master Silas. " When the ale hath done with its humming, it is time, methinks, to dismiss it. Sir, there never was any more: you might as well ask for more after Amen or the see of Canterbury."

Sir Thomas was dissatisfied, and turned off the discourse; and peradventure he grew more inclined to be gracious unto Willy from the slight rub his chaplain had given him, were it only for the contrariety. When he had collected his thoughts, he was determined to assert his supremacy on the score of poetry.

" Deans, I perceive, like other quality," said he, " cannot run on long together. My friend, Sir Everard Starkeye could never over-leap four bars. I remember but one composition of his; on a young lady who mocked at his inconsistency, in calling her sometimes his Grace and at other times his Muse.

> " My Grace shall Fanny Carew be,
>   While here she deigns to stay;
> And (ah, how sad the change for me!)
>   My Muse when far away!"

And when we laughed at him for turning his back upon her after the fourth verse, all he could say for himself was, that he would rather a game at *all fours* with Fanny, than *ombre* and *picquet* with the finest furbelows in

Christendom. Men of condition do usually want a belt in the course."

Whereunto said Master Silas,

" Men out of condition are quite as liable to lack it, methinks."

" Silas! Silas!" replied the knight, impatiently, " prythee keep to thy divinity, thy strong hold upon Zion ; thence none that faces thee can draw thee without being bitten to the bone. Leave poetry to me."

" With all my heart," quoth Master Silas, " I will never ask a belt from her, until I see she can afford to give a shirt. She has promised a belt, indeed, not one, however, that doth much improve the wind, to this lad here, and will keep her word ; but she was forced to borrow the pattern from a Carthusian friar, and somehow it slips above the shoulder."

" I am by no means sure of that," quoth Sir Thomas. " He shall have fair play. He carrieth in his mind many valuable things, whereof it hath pleased Providence to ordain

him the depository.   He hath laid before us
certain sprigs of poetry from Oxford, trim as
pennyroyal, and larger leaves of household
divinity, the most mildly-savoured ; pleasant
in health, and wholesome in sickness."

" I relish not such mutton-broth divinity,"
said Master Silas.   " It makes me sick in
" order to settle my stomach."

" We may improve it," said the knight,
" but first let us hear more."

Then did William Shakspeare resume Dr.
Glaston's discourse.

" ' Ethelbert! I think thou walkest but
little ; otherwise I should take thee with me,
some fine fresh morning, as far as unto the
first hamlet on the Cherwell.   There lies
young Wellerby, who, the year before, was
wont to pass many hours of the day poetising
amidst the ruins of Godgson nunnery.   It is
said that he bore a fondness toward a young
maiden in that place, formerly a village, now
containing but two old farm-houses.   In my

memory there were still extant several dormi-
tories. Some love-sick girl had recollected
an ancient name, and had engraven on a stone
with a garden-nail, which lay in rust near it,

POORE ROSAMUND.

I entered these precincts, and beheld a youth
of manly form and countenance, washing and
wiping a stone with a handful of wet grass;
and on my going up to him, and asking
what he had found, he shewed it to me The
next time I saw him was near the banks of
the Cherwell. He had tried, it appears, to
forget or overcome his foolish passion, and
had applied his whole mind unto study.
He was foiled by his competitor; and now
he sought consolation in poetry. Whether
this opened the wounds that had closed in his
youthful breast, and malignant Love, in his
revenge, poisoned it; or whether the disappointment he had experienced in finding
others preferred to him, first in the paths of

fortune, then in those of the muses,—he was thought to have died broken-hearted.

"'About half a mile from St. John's College is the termination of a natural terrace, with the Cherwell close under it, in some places bright with yellow and red flowers glancing and glowing through the stream, and suddenly in others dark with the shadows of many different trees, in broad overbending thickets, and with rushes spear-high, and party-coloured flags.

"'After a walk in Midsummer, the immersion of our hands into the cool and closing grass is surely not the least among our animal delights. I was just seated, and the first sensation of rest vibrated in me gently, as though it were music to the limbs, when I discoverd by a hollow in the herbage that another was near. The long meadow-sweet and blooming burnet half concealed from me him whom the earth was about to hide totally and for ever.

"'Master Batchelor!' said I, 'it is ill-sleeping by the water-side.'

" ' No answer was returned. I arose, went to the place, and recognised poor Wellerby. His brow was moist, his cheek was warm. A few moments earlier, and that dismal lake whereunto and wherefrom the waters of life, the buoyant blood, ran no longer, might have received one vivifying ray reflected from my poor casement. I might not indeed have comforted—I have often failed : but there is one who never has; and the strengthener of the bruised reed should have been with us.

" ' Remembering that his mother did abide one mile further on, I walked forward to the mansion, and asked her what tidings she lately had received of her son. She replied, that having given up his mind to light studies, the fellows of the college would not elect him. The master had warned him before-hand to abandon his selfish poetry, take up manfully the quarterstaff of logic, and wield it for St. John's, come who would into the ring. " We want our man," said he to me, " and your son hath failed us in the hour of need.   Madam, he hath been foully beaten in the schools by one he might have swallowed, with due exercise."

" ' I rated him, told him I was poor, and he knew it. He was stung, and threw himself upon my neck, and wept. Twelve days have passed since, and only three rainy ones. I hear he has been seen upon the knoll yonder, but hither he hath not come. I trust he knows at last the value of time, and I shall be heartily glad to see him after this accession of know-ledge. Twelve days, it is true, are rather a chink than a gap in time; yet, O gentle sir! they are that chink which makes the vase quite valueless. There are light words which may never be shaken off the mind they fall on. My child, who was hurt by me, will not let me see the marks.'

" ' Lady!' said I, ' none are left upon him. Be comforted! thou shalt see him this hour. All that thy God hath not taken is yet thine.' She looked at me earnestly, and would have

then asked something, but her voice failed her.
There was no agony, no motion, save in the
lips and cheeks.   Being the widow of one who
fought under Hawkins, she remembered his
courage and sustained the shock, and said
calmly, ' God's will be done!   I pray that he
find me as worthy as he findeth me willing to
join them.'

" Now, in her unearthly thoughts, she had
led her only son to the bosom of her husband ;
and in her spirit (which often is permitted to
pass the gates of death with holy love) she left
them both with their Creator.

" The curate of the village sent those who
should bring home the body ; and some days
afterwards he came unto me, beseeching me to
write the epitaph.   Being no friend to stone-
cutter's charges, I entered not into biography,
but wrote these few words :

' JOANNES WELLERBY,

LITERARUM QUÆSIVIT GLORIAM,

VIDET DEI.' "

" Poor Jack! poor Jack!" sourly quoth Master Silas. " If your wise doctor could say nothing more about the fool, who died like a rotten sheep among the darnels, his Latin might have held out for the father, and might have told people he was as cool as a cucumber at home, and as hot as pepper in battle. Could he not find room enough on the whinstone, to tell the folks of the village how he played the devil among the dons, burning their fingers when they would put thumbscrews upon us, punching them in the wesand as a blacksmith punches a horse-shoe, and throwing them overboard like bilgewater?

" Has Oxford lost all her Latin? Here is no *capitani filius;* no more mention of family than a Welchman would have allowed him; no *hic jacet;* and, worse than all, the devil a tittle of *spe redemptionis,* or *anno Domini.*"

" Willy!" quoth Sir Thomas, " I shrewdly do suspect there was more, and that thou hast forgotten it."

" Sir!" answered Willy, " I wrote not down the words, fearing to mis-spell them, and begged them of the doctor, when I took my leave of him on the morrow; and verily he wrote down all he had repeated. I keep them always in the tin-box in my waistcoat-pocket, among the eel-hooks, on a scrap of paper a finger's length and breadth, folded in the middle to fit. And when the eels are running, I often take it out and read it before I am aware. I could as soon forget my own epitaph as this."

" Simpleton!" said Sir Thomas, with his gentle compassionate smile; " but thou hast cleared thyself."

SIR SILAS.

" I think the doctor gave one idle chap as much solid pudding as he could digest, with a slice to spare for another."

WILLIAM SHAKSPEARE.

" And yet after this pudding the doctor gave him a spoonful of custard, flavoured with

a little bitter, which was mostly left at the bottom for the other idle chap."

Sir Thomas not only did endure this very
goodnaturedly, but deigned even to take in
good part the smile upon my countenance, as
though he were a smile-collector, and as though
his estate were so humble that he could hold
his laced-bonnet (in all his bravery) for bear
and fiddle.

He then said unto Willy,

" Place likewise this custard before us."

" There is but little of it; the platter is
shallow," replied he; " 'twas suited to Master
Ethelbert's appetite. The contents were these :

" ' The things whereon thy whole soul
brooded in its innermost recesses, and with all
its warmth and energy, will pass unprised and
unregarded, not only throughout thy lifetime
but long after. For the higher beauties of
poetry are beyond the capacity, beyond the
vision of almost all. Once perhaps in half a
century a single star is discovered, then named

and registered, then mentioned by five studious men to five more; at last some twenty say, or repeat in writing, what they have heard about it. Other stars await other discoveries. Few and solitary, and wide asunder, are those who calculate their relative distances, their mysterious influences, their glorious magnitude, and their stupendous height. 'Tis so, believe me, and ever was so, with the truest and best poetry. Homer, they say, was blind; he might have been ere he died; that he sat among the blind, we are sure.

" ' Happy they who, like this young lad from Stratford, write poetry on the saddle-bow when their geldings are jaded, and keep the desk for better purposes.'

" The young gentlemen, like the elderly, all turned their faces toward me, to my confusion, so much did I remark of sneer and scoff at my cost. Master Ethelbert was the only one who spared me. He smiled and said,

" ' Be patient! From the higher heavens

of poetry, it is long before the radiance of the brightest star can reach the world below. We hear that one man finds out one beauty, another man finds out another, placing his observatory and instruments on the poet's grave. The worms must have eaten us before it is rightly known what we are. It is only when we are skeletons that we are boxed and ticketed, and prised and shewn. Be it so! I shall not be tired of waiting.'"

"Reasonable youth!" said Sir Thomas; "yet both he and Glaston walk rather *a straddle*, methinks. They might have stepped up to thee more straightforwardly, and told thee the trade ill suiteth thee, having little fire, little fantasy, and little learning. Furthermore, that one poet as one bull sufficeth for two parishes, and that, where they are stuck too close together, they are apt to fire, like haystacks. I have known it myself: I have had my malignants and scoffers."

WILLIAM SHAKSPEARE.

"I never could have thought it."

SIR THOMAS.

" There again! Another proof of thy inexperience."

WILLIAM SHAKSPEARE.

" Matt Atterend! Matt Atterend! where wert thou sleeping!"

SIR THOMAS.

" I shall now from my own stores impart unto thee what will avail to tame thee, shewing the utter hopelessness of standing on that golden weathercock which supporteth but one at a time.

" The passion for poetry wherewith Monsieur Dubois would have inspired me, as he was bound to do, being paid before-hand, had cold water thrown upon it by that unlucky one, Sir Everard. He ridiculed the idea of male and female rhymes, and the necessity of trying them as rigidly by the eye as by the ear ; saying to Monsieur Dubois that the palate, in which the French excel all mortals, ought also to be consulted in their acceptance or rejection. Monsieur Dubois told us that if we did not wish to be taught French verse, he would teach us English. Sir Everard preferred the Greek; but Monsieur Dubois would not engage to teach the mysteries of that poetry in fewer than thirty lessons, having (since his misfortunes) forgotten the letters and some other necessaries.

" The first poem I ever wrote was in the character of a shepherd, to Mistress Anne Nanfan, daughter of Squire Fulke Nanfan, of Worcestershire, at that time on a visit to the worshipful family of Compton at Long Compton.

" We were young creatures; I but twenty-four and seven months (for it was written on the 14th of May), and she well-nigh upon a twelvemonth younger. My own verses, the first, are neither here nor there; indeed, they were imbedded in solid prose, like lampreys and ram's-horns* in our limestone, and would be hard to get out whole. What they are may be seen by her answer, all in verse:

* It is doubtful whether Doctor Buckland will agree with Sir Thomas that these petrifactions are ram's-horns and lampreys.

> " ' Faithful shepherd ! dearest Tommy !
>   I have received the letter from ye,
>   And mightily delight therein.
>   But mother, *she* says, " Nanny ! Nanny !
>   *How, being staid and prudent, can ye*
>   *Think of a man and not of sin ?*"

> " ' Sir shepherd ! I held down my head,
>   And " *Mother ! fie for shame !*" I said ;
>   All I could say would not content her ;
>   Mother she would for ever harp on't,
>   " *A man's no better than a sarpent,*
>   *And not a crumb more innocenter.*" '

" I know not how it happeneth," said the knight, " but a poet doth open before a poet, albeit of baser sort. It is not that I hold my poetry to be better than some other in time past, it is because I would shew thee that I was virtuous and wooed virtuously, that I repeat it. Furthermore, I wished to leave a deep impression on the mother's mind that she was exceedingly wrong in doubting my innocence."

WILLIAM SHAKSPEARE.

" Gracious Heaven ! and was this too doubted ?"

SIR THOMAS.

" Maybe not ; but the whole race of men, the whole male sex, wanted and found in me a protector. I shewed her what I was ready to do."

WILLIAM SHAKSPEARE.

" Perhaps, sir, it was for that very thing that she put the daughter back and herself forward."

SIR THOMAS.

" I say not so, but thou mayest know as much as befitteth, as follows :

  ' Worshipful lady ! honoured madam !
  I at this present truly glad am
      To have so fair an opportunity
  Of saying I would be the man
  To bind in wedlock Mistress Anne,
      Living with her in holy unity.

  ' And for a jointure I will gi'e her
  A good two hundred pounds a-year
      Accruing from my landed rents,
  Whereof see t'other paper, telling
  'Lands, copses, and grown woods for felling,
      Capons, and cottage tenements.

‘ And who must come at sound of horn,
And who pays but a barley-corn,
    And who is bound to keep a whelp,
And what is brought me for the pound,
And copyholders, which are sound,
    And which do need the leech's help.

‘ And you may see in these two pages
Exact their illnesses and ages,
    Enough (God willing) to content ye;
Who looks full red, who looks full yellow,
Who plies the mullen, who the mallow,
    Who fails at fifty, who at twenty.

‘ Jim Yates must go; he's one day very hot
And one day ice; I take a heriot;
    And poorly, poorly's Jacob Burgess.
The doctor tells me he has pour'd
Into his stomach half his hoard
    Of anthelminticals and purges.

‘ Judith, the wife of Ebenezer
Fillpots, won't have him long to teaze her;
    Fillpots blows hot and cold like Jim,
And, sleepless lest the boys should plunder
His orchard, he must soon knock under;
    Death has been looking out for him.

‘ He blusters; but his good yard land
Under the church, his ale-house, and
    His Bible, which he cut in spite,

Must all fall in; he stamps and swears
And sets his neighbours by the ears—
  Fillpots! thy saddle sits not tight!'

" The epitaph is ready:

    ' *Here*
Lies one whom all his friends did fear
  More than they ever feared the Lord:
In peace, he was at times a Christian;
In strife, what stubboner Philistine!
  Sing, sing his psalm with one accord.

' And he who lent my lord his wife
Has but a very ticklish life;
  Although she won him many a hundred,
'Twon't do; none comes with briefs and wills,
And all her gainings are gilt pills
  From the sick madman that she plundered.

' And the brave lad who sent the bluff
Olive-faced Frenchman (sure enough)
  Screaming and scouring like a plover,
Must follow — him I mean who dash'd
Into the water, and then thrash'd
  The cullion past the town of Dover.

' But first there goes the blear old dame
Who nurs'd me; you have heard her name,
  No doubt, at Compton, Sarah Salways;

There are twelve groats at once, beside
The frying-pan in which she fried
Her pancakes.

Madam, I am always, &c.

T. L.'

" I did believe that such a clear and con-
scientious exposure of my affairs would have
brought me a like return. My letter was sent
back to me with small courtesy. It may be
there was no paper in the house, or none equal-
ling mine in whiteness. No notice was taken
of the rent-roll; but between the second and
third stanza these four lines were written, in a
very fine hand:

' Most honor'd knight, Sir Thomas! two
For merry Nan will never do;
Now under favour let me say 't,
She will bring more herself than that.'

I have reason to believe that the worthy lady
did neither write nor countenance the same,
perhaps did not ever know of them. She
always had at her elbow one who jogged it

when he listed, and, although he could not overrule the daughter, he took especial care that none other should remove her from his tutelage, even when she had fairly grown up to woman's estate.

" Now, after all this condescension and confidence, promise me, good lad, promise that thou wilt not edge and elbow me. Never let it be said, when people say, *Sir Thomas was a poet when he willed it; so is Bill Shakspeare!* It beseemeth not that our names do go together cheek by jowl in this familiar fashion, like an old beagle and a whelp, in couples, where if the one would, the other would not."

SIR SILAS.

" Sir, while these thoughts are passing in your mind, remember there is another pair of couples out of which it would be as well to keep the cur's neck."

SIR THOMAS.

" Young man! dost thou understand Master Silas?"

WILLIAM SHAKSPEARE.

" But too well.   Not those couples in which it might be apprehended that your worship and my unworthiness should appear too close together; but those sorrowfuller which peradventure might unite Master Silas and me in our road to Warwick and upwards. But I resign all right and title unto these as willingly as I did unto the other, and am as ready to let him go alone."

SIR SILAS.

" If we keep wheeling and wheeling, like a flock of pigeons, and rising again when we are within a foot of the ground, we shall never fill the craw."

SIR THOMAS.

" Do thou then question him, Silas?"

SIR SILAS.

" I am none of the quorum: the business is none of mine."

Then Sir Thomas took Master Silas again into the bay-window, and said softly,

" Silas, he hath no inkling of thy meaning. The business is a ticklish one.   I like not over-much to meddle and make therein."

Master Silas stood dissatisfied awhile, and then answered,

" The girl's mother, sir, was housemaid and sempstress in your own family, time back, and you thereby have a right over her unto the third and fourth generation."

" I may have, Silas," said his worship, " but it was no longer than four or five years agone that folks were fain to speak maliciously of me for only finding my horse in her hovel."

Sir Silas looked red and shiny as a ripe strawberry on a Snitterfield tile, and answered somewhat peevishly,

" The same folks, I misgive me, may find the rogue's there any night in the week."

Whereunto replied Sir Thomas, mortifiedly,

" I cannot think it, Silas! I cannot think it."

And after some hesitation and disquiet,

" Nay, I am resolved I will not think it: no man, friend or enemy, shall push it into me."

" Worshipful sir!" answered Master Silas, " I am as resolute as any one in what I would think and what I would not think, and never was known to fight dunghill in either cockpit.

" Were he only out of the way, she might do her duty, but what doth she now?

" She points his young beard for him ; persuades him it grows thicker and thicker, blacker and blacker ; she washes his ruff, stiffens it, plaits it, tries it upon his neck, removes the hair from under it, pinches it with thumb and forefinger, pretending that he hath moiled it, puts her hand all the way round it, *setting it to rights*, as she calleth it...

" Ah, Sir Thomas ! a louder whistle than that will never call her back again when she is off with him."

Sir Thomas was angered, and cried tartly,

" Who whistled ? I would know."

Master Silas said submissively,

" Your honour, as wrongfully I fancied."

" Wrongfully, indeed, and to my no small disparagement and discomfort," said the knight, verily believing that he had not whistled; for deep and dubious were his cogitations.

" I protest," went he on to say, " I protest it was the wind of the casement; and if I live another year I will put a better in the place of it... Whistle indeed! for what? I care no more about her than about an unfledged cygnet ... a child,* a chicken, a mere kitten, a crab-blossom in the hedge."

The dignity of his worship was wounded by Master Silas unaware, and his wrath again turned suddenly upon poor William.

" Hark-ye, knave! hark-ye again, ill-looking stripling, lanky from vicious courses! I

* She was then twenty-seven years of age. Sir Thomas must have spoken of her from earlier recollections. Shakspeare was in the twentieth year.

will reclaim thee from them : I will do what thy own father would, and cannot. Thou shalt follow his business."

" I cannot do better, may it please your worship!" said the lad.

" It shall lead thee unto wealth and respectability," said the knight, somewhat appeased by his ready compliancy and low gentle voice. " Yea, but not here; no witches, no wantons (this word fell gravely and at full-length upon the ear), no spells hereabout.

" Gloucestershire is within a measured mile of thy dwelling. There is one at Bristol, formerly a parish-boy, or little better, who now writeth himself *gentleman* in large round letters, and hath been elected, I hear, to serve as burgess in parliament for his native city; just as though he had eaten a capon or turkey-poult in his youth, and had actually been at grammar-school and college. When he began, he had not credit for a goat-skin; and now, behold ye! this very coat upon my back did cost me eight shillings the dearer for him, he bought up wool so largely.":

WILLIAM SHAKSPEARE.

" May it please your worship! if my father so ordereth, I go cheerfully."

SIR THOMAS.

" Thou art grown discreet and dutiful : I am fain to command thy release, taking thy promise on oath, and some reasonable security, that thou wilt abstain and withhold in future from that idle and silly slut, that sly and scoffing giggler, Hannah Hathaway, with whom, to the heart-ache of thy poor worthy father, thou wantonly keepest company."

Then did Sir Thomas ask Master Silas Gough for the Book of Life, bidding him deliver it into the right hand of Billy, with an eye upon him that he touch it with both lips; it being taught by the Jesuits, and caught too greedily out of their society and communion, that whoso toucheth it with one lip only, and thereafter sweareth falsely, cannot be called a perjurer, since perjury is breaking an oath. But breaking half an oath, as he doth who toucheth the Bible or crucifix with one lip only, is no more perjury than breaking an eggshell is breaking an egg, the shell being a part, and the egg being an integral.

William did take the Holy Book with all due reverence the instant it was offered to his hand. His stature seemed to rise therefrom as from a pulpit, and Sir Thomas was quite edified.

" Obedient and conducible youth!" said he. " See there, Master Silas! what hast thou now to say against him? who sees farthest?"

" The man from the gallows is the most likely, bating his nightcap and blinker," said Master Silas peevishly. " He hath not out-witted me yet."

" He seized upon the Anchor of Faith like a martyr," said Sir Thomas, " and even now his face burns red as elder-wine before the gossips."

WILLIAM SHAKSPEARE.

" I await the further orders of your worship from the chair."

SIR THOMAS.

" I return and seat myself."

And then did Sir Thomas say with great complacency and satisfaction in the ear of Master Silas,

" What civility, and deference, and sedateness of mind, Silas !"

But Master Silas answered not.

WILLIAM SHAKSPEARE.

" Must I swear, sir ?"

SIR THOMAS.

" Yea, swear; be of good courage. I protest to thee by my honour and knighthood, no ill shall come unto thee therefrom. Thou shalt not be circumvented in thy simpleness and inexperience."

Willy, having taken the Book of Life,

did kiss it piously, and did press it unto his breast, saying,

" Tenderest love is the growth of my heart, as the grass is of Alvescote mead.

" May I lose my life or my friends, or my memory, or my reason ; may I be viler in my own eyes than those men are " . . . . .

Here he was interrupted, most lovingly, by Sir Thomas, who said unto him,

" Nay, nay, nay! poor youth! do not tell me so! they are not such very bad men ; since thou appealest unto Cæsar ; that is, unto the judgment-seat."

Now his worship did mean the two witnesses, Joseph and Euseby ; and, sooth to say, there be many worse. But William had them not in his eye ; his thoughts were elsewhere, as will be evident,— for he went on thus :—

. . . . " If ever I forget or desert thee, or ever cease to worship* and cherish thee, my Hannah !"

---

* It is to be feared that his taste for venison outlasted that for matrimony, spite of this vow.

SIR SILAS.

" The madman! the audacious, desperate, outrageous villain! Look-ye, sir! where he flung the Holy Gospel! Behold it on the holly and box boughs in the chimney-place, spreaden all abroad, like a lad about to be whipt!"

SIR THOMAS.

" Miscreant knave! I will send after him forthwith!

" Ho, there! is the caitiff at hand, or running off?"

Jonas Greenfield the butler did budge forward after a while, and say, on being questioned,

" Surely, that was he! Was his nag tied to the iron gate at the lodge, Master Silas?"

SIR SILAS.

" What should I know about a thief's nag, Jonas Greenfield?"

" And didst thou let him go, Jonas? even

thou?" said Sir Thomas. "What! are none found faithful?"

"Lord love your worship," said Jonas Greenfield; "a man of threescore and two may miss catching a kite upon wing. Fleetness doth not make folks the faithfuller, or that youth yonder beats us all in faithfulness.

"Look! he darts on like a greyhound whelp after a leveret. He, sure enough, it was! I now remember the sorrel mare his father bought of John Kinderley last Lammas, swift as he threaded the trees along the park. He must have reached Wellesbourne ere now at that gallop, and pretty nigh Walton-hill."

SIR THOMAS.

"Merciful Christ! grant the country be rid of him for ever! What dishonour upon his friends and native town! A reputable woolstapler's son turned gipsy and poet for life."

SIR SILAS.

"A Beelzebub; he spake as bigly and fiercely as a soaken yeoman at an election feast . . . . this obedient and conducible youth!"

SIR THOMAS.

" It was so written. Hold thy peace, Silas."

LAUS DEO.

E. B.

[illegible]

[illegible]

[illegible]

[illegible]

[illegible]

[illegible]

[illegible]

[illegible]

[illegible]

feast . . . . this obedient and conducible youth!"

"It was so written. Hold thy peace, Silas!"

LAUS DEO.

E. B.

POST-SCRIPTUM

BY ME EPHRAIM BARNETT.

TWELVE days are over and gone since William Shakspeare did leave our parts. And the spinster, Hannah Hathaway, is in sad doleful plight about him; forasmuch as Master Silas Gough went yesterday unto her, in her mother's house at Shottery, and did desire both her and her mother to take heed and be admonished, that if ever she, Hannah, threw away one thought after the runagate William Shakspeare, he should swing.

M

The girl could do nothing but weep; while as the mother did give her solemn promise that her daughter should never more think about him all her natural life, reckoning from the moment of this her promise.

And the maiden, now growing more reasonable, did promise the same. But Master Silas said,

"*I doubt you will, though.*"

"No," said the mother, "*I answer for her she shall not think of him, even if she see his ghost.*"

Hannah screamed, and swooned, the better to forget him. And Master Silas went home easier and contenteder. For now all the worst of his hard duty was accomplished; he having been, on the Wednesday of last week, at the speech of Master John Shakspeare, Will's father, to inquire whether the sorrel mare was his. To which question the said Master John Shakspeare did answer, "*Yea.*"

"*Enough said!*" rejoined Master Silas.

" Horse-stealing is capital. We shall bind thee over to appear against the culprit, as prosecutor, at the next assizes."

May the Lord in his mercy give the lad a good deliverance, if so be it be no sin to wish it!

October 1, A.D. 1582.

LAUS DEO.

EDITOR'S APOLOGY.

A PART only of the many deficiencies which the reader will discover in this volume is attributable to the Editor. These, however, it is his duty to account for, and he will do it as briefly as he can.

The *facsimiles* (as printers' boys call them, meaning *specimens*) of the handwriting of nearly all the persons introduced, might perhaps have been procured, had sufficient time been allowed for another journey into Warwickshire. That of Shakspeare is known already in the signature to his will, but deformed by sickness: that of Sir Thomas Lacy is extant at the bottom of a commitment of a female vagrant, for having a sucking child in her arms on the public road: that of Silas Gough is affixed to the register of births and marriages, during several years, in the parishes of Hampton Lucy and Charlecote, and certifies one death — that of Euseby Treen—surmised, at least, to be Euseby Treen, in the letters E. T. cut on a bench seven inches thick, under an old pollard-oak outside the park - paling of Charlecote, towards the north-east. For this discovery the Editor is indebted to a most respectable and intelligent farmer in the adjoining parish of Wasperton, in which parish Treen's elder brother lies buried. The worthy farmer is unwilling to accept the large portion of fame justly due to him for the services he has thus rendered to literature in elucidating the history of Shakspeare and his times. The Editor is unable to render adequate thanks to the Rev. Stephen Turnover, for the gratification he received in his curious library by a sight of Joseph Carnaby's name at full length, in red ink, coming from a trumpet in the mouth of an angel. This invaluable document is upon an engraving in a frontispiece to the New Testament.

But as unhappily he could procure no signature of Hannah Hathaway, nor of her mother, and only a questionable one of Mr. John Shakpeare, the poet's father, there being two, in two very different hands,— both he and the Publisher were of opinion that the graphical part of the volume would be justly censured as extremely incomplete, and that what we could give would only raise inextinguishable regret for that which we could not. On this reflection all have been omitted.

The Editor and Publisher are unwilling to affix any mark of disapprobation on the very clever engraver who undertook the sorrel mare; but as, in the memorable words of that ingenious gentleman from Ireland, whose polished and elaborate epigrams raised him justly to the rank of prime minister,

" White was not *so very* white ;"

in like manner it appeared to nearly all the artists we consulted, that the sorrel mare was not *so sorrel* in print.

Such are the reasons why the little volume here laid before the public is defective in those decorations which the exalted state of literature demands.

A CONFERENCE

OF

MASTER EDMUND SPENSER,

A GENTLEMAN OF NOTE,

WITH

THE EARL OF ESSEX,

TOUCHING

THE STATE OF IRELAND,

ANNO. DOM. 1598.

PREFACE.

To the same worthy man who preserved the *Examination of Shakspeare,*
we are indebted for what he entitles on
the cover, *A Conference of Master Edmund Spenser, &c., with the Earl of
Essex.* It must be confessed that this
Conference throws little light upon the
great rebellion of Ireland.   Nevertheless,
there are some curious minds, which,
perhaps, may take an interest in the
conversation of two illustrious men, one
distinguished by his genius, the other
by the favour of his sovereign.   The
Editor, it will be perceived, is but little
practised in the ways of literature, much
less is he gifted with that prophetic spirit

which can anticipate the judgment of the public. It may be that he is too idle or too apathetic to think anxiously or much about the matter; and yet he has been amused, in his earlier days, at watching the first appearance of such few books as he believed to be the production of some powerful intellect. He has seen people slowly rise up to them, like carp in a pond when food is thrown among them; some of which carp snatch suddenly at a morsel, and swallow it; others touch it gently with their barbe, pass deliberately by, and leave it; others wriggle and rub against it more disdainfully; others, in sober truth, know not what to make of it, swim round and round it, eye it on the sunny side, eye it on the shady; approach it, question it, shoulder it, flap it with the tail, turn it over, look askance at it, take a pea-shell or a worm instead of it, and plunge again their contented heads into the comfortable mud: after some seasons the same food will suit their stomachs better.

The Editor has seen all this, and been an actor in it, whether at Chantilly or Fontainebleau is indifferent to the reader; and it has occurred to him that Shakspeare and Spenser were thrown among such carp, and began to be relished (the worst, of course, first) after many years. He is certain that these two publications can interest only the antiquary and biographer; enough if even such find their account in them.

IT happened by mere accident that so obscure a man as Ephraim Barnett, with no peculiar zeal for genius, and with no other scope or intention than a lesson for his descendants, has preserved an authentic memorial of the principal event both in the life of Shakspeare and of Spenser : the one event was very near the cause of terminating Shakspeare's, the other did terminate Spenser's. He accounts for his knowledge of the facts naturally enough, as those will readily admit who have the patience to read his paper on the subject. It would be inhumane in the Editor to ask any of it for himself, when it is about to undergo such an exertion.

ESSEX AND SPENSER.

ESSEX.

" Instantly on hearing of thy arrival from Ireland, I sent a message to thee, good Edmund, that I might learn from one so judicious and dispassionate as thou art, the real state of things in that distracted country; it having pleased the queen's majesty to think of appointing me her deputy, in order to bring the rebellious to submission."

SPENSER.

" Wisely and well considered; but more worthily of her judgment than her affection. May your lordship overcome, as you have ever done, the difficulties and dangers you foresee."

ESSEX.

" We grow weak by striking at random; and knowing that I must strike, and strike heavily, I would fain see exactly where the stroke shall fall.

" Some attribute to the Irish all sorts of excesses; others tell us that these are old stories; that there is not a more inoffensive race of merry creatures under heaven, and that their crimes are all hatched for them here in England, by the incubation of printers' boys, and are brought to market at times of distressing dearth in news.   From all that I myself have seen of them, I can only say, that the civilised (I mean the richer and titled) are as susceptible of heat as iron, and as impenetrable to light as granite.   The half-barbarous are probably worse; the utterly barbarous may be somewhat better.   Like game-cocks, they must spur when they meet.   One fights because he fights an Englishman; another because the fellow he quarrels with comes from a distant county; a third because the next parish is an eyesore to him, and his fist-mate is from it. The only thing in which they all agree as proper law is the tooth-for-tooth act. Luckily we have a bishop who is a native, and we called him before the queen. He represented to her majesty, that every thing in Old Ireland tended to re-produce its kind; crimes among others; and he declared frankly, that if an honest man is murdered, or what is dearer to an honest man, if his honour is wounded in the person of his wife, it must be expected that he will retaliate. Her majesty delivered it as her opinion, that the latter case of vindictiveness was more likely to take effect than the former. But the bishop replied, that in his conscience he could not answer for either if the man was up. The dean of the same diocese gave us a more favourable report. Being a justice of the peace, he averred most solemnly that no man ever had complained to him of murder, excepting one who had lost so many fore-teeth by a cudgel that his deposition could not be taken exactly, added to which, his head was a little clouded with drunkenness; furthermore, that extremely few women had adduced sufficiently clear proofs of violence, excepting those who were wilful and resisted with tooth and nail. In all which cases it was difficult, nay impossible, to ascertain which violence began first and lasted longest.

" There is not a nation upon earth that pretends to be so superlatively generous and high-minded; and there is not one, (I speak from experience) so utterly base and venal. I have positive proof that the nobility, in a mass, are agreed to sell, for a stipulated sum, all their rights and privileges, so much per man; and the queen is inclined thereunto. But would our parliament consent to pay money for a cargo of rotten pilchards? And would not our captains be readier to swamp than to import them? The noisiest rogues in our kingdom, if not quieted by a halter, may be quieted by making them brief-collectors, and by allowing them first to encourage the incendiary, then to denounce and hang him, and lastly to collect all the money they can, running up and down with the whining ferocity of half-starved hyænas, under pretence of repairing the damages their exhausted country hath sustained. Others ask modestly a few thousands a-year, and no more, from those whom they represent to us as naked and famished; and prove clearly to every dispassionate man who hath a single drop of free blood in his veins, that at least this pittance is due to them for abandoning their liberal and lucrative professions, and for endangering their valuable lives on the tempestuous seas, in order that the voice of Truth may sound for once upon the shores of England, and Humanity cast her shadow on the council-chamber.

"I gave a dinner to a party of these

fellows a few weeks ago. I know not how
many kings and princes were amongst them,
nor how many poets, and prophets, and legis-
lators, and sages. When they were half-
drunk, they coaxed and threatened; when
they had gone somewhat deeper, they joked,
and croaked, and hiccupped, and wept over
sweet Ireland; and when they could neither
stand nor sit any longer, they fell upon their
knees and their noddles, and swore that limbs,
life, liberty, Ireland, and God himself, were
all at the queen's service. It was only their
holy religion—the religion of their forefathers
.... here sobs interrupted some, howls
others, execrations more, and the liquor they
had ingulfed the rest. I looked down on
them with stupor and astonishment, seeing
faces, forms, dresses, much like ours, and recol-
lecting their ignorance, levity, and ferocity.
My pages drew them gently by the heels down
the steps; my grooms set them upright (inasmuch as might be) on their horses; and the

people in the streets, shouting and pelting, sent forward the beasts to their straw.

" Various plans have been laid before us for civilising or coercing them. Among the pacific, it was proposed to make an offer to five hundred of the richer Jews in the Hanse-towns and in Poland, who should be raised to the dignity of the Irish peerage, and endowed with four thousand acres of good forfeited land, on condition of paying each two thousand pounds, and of keeping up ten horsemen and twenty foot, Germans or Poles, in readiness for service.

" The Catholics bear no where such ill will towards Jews as towards Protestants. Brooks make even worse neighbours than oceans do.

" I myself saw no objection to the measure: but our gracious queen declared she had an insuperable one — *they stank!* We all acknowledged the strength of the argument, and took out our handkerchiefs. Lord Burleigh almost fainted; and Raleigh wondered how the Emperor Titus could bring up his men against Jerusalem.

"'Ah!' said he, looking reverentially at her majesty, 'the star of Berenice shone above him! and what evil influence could that star not quell! what malignancy could it not annihilate!'

"Hereupon he touched the earth with his brow, until the queen said,

"'Sir Walter! lift me up those laurels.'

"At which manifestation of princely good-will he was advancing to kiss her majesty's hand, but she waved it, and said sharply,

"'Stand there, dog!'

"Now what tale have you for us?

SPENSER.

"Interrogate me, my lord, that I may answer each question distinctly, my mind being in utter confusion at what I have seen and undergone."

ESSEX.

" Give me thy account and opinion of these very affairs as thou leftest them; for I would rather know one part well, than all imperfectly; and the violences of which I have heard within the day surpass belief.

" Why weepest thou, my gentle Spenser? Have the rebels sacked thy house?"

SPENSER.

" They have plundered and utterly destroyed it."

ESSEX.

" I grieve for thee, and will see thee righted."

SPENSER.

" In this they have little harmed me."

ESSEX.

" How! I have heard it reported that thy grounds are fertile and thy mansion* large and pleasant."

* It was purchased, about half a century ago, by a victualler and banker, one Tonson, the father or grandfather of Lord Riversdale.

SPENSER.

" If river, and lake, and meadow-ground, and mountain, could render any place the abode of pleasantness, pleasant was mine, indeed !

" On the lovely banks of Mulla I found deep contentment. Under the dark alders did I muse and meditate. Innocent hopes were my gravest cares, and my playfullest fancy was with kindly wishes. Ah! surely of all cruelties the worst is to extinguish our kindness. Mine is gone : I love the people and the land no longer. My lord, ask me not about them ; I may speak injuriously."

ESSEX.

" Think rather, then, of thy happier hours and busier occupations ; these likewise may instruct me."

SPENSER.

" The first seeds I sowed in the garden, ere the old castle was made habitable for my lovely bride, were acorns from Penshurst. I planted a little oak before my mansion at the birth of each child. My sons, I said to myself, shall often play in the shade of them when I am gone, and every year shall they take the measure of their growth, as fondly as I take theirs."

ESSEX.

" Well, well; but let not this thought make thee weep so bitterly."

SPENSER.

" Poison may ooze from beautiful plants; deadly grief from dearest reminiscences.

" I *must* grieve, I *must* weep: it seems the law of God, and the only one that men are not disposed to controvert. In the performance of this alone do they effectually aid one another."

ESSEX.

" Spenser! I wish I had at hand any arguments or persuasions of force sufficient to remove thy sorrow: but really I am not in

N

the habit of seeing men grieve at any thing, except the loss of favour at court, or of a hawk, or of a buck-hound. And were I to swear out my condolences to a man of thy discernment, in the same round, roll-call phrases we employ with one another upon these occasions, I should be guilty, not of insincerity but of insolence. True grief hath ever something sacred in it; and when it visiteth a wise man and a brave one, is most holy.

"Nay, kiss not my hand: he whom God smiteth hath God with him. In his presence what am I?"

SPENSER.

"Never so great, my lord, as at this hour, when you see aright who is greater. May He guide your counsels, and preserve your life and glory!"

ESSEX.

"Where are thy friends? Are they with thee?"

SPENSER.

" Ah, where, indeed! Generous, true-hearted Philip! where art thou! whose presence was unto me peace and safety; whose smile was contentment, and whose praise renown. My lord! I cannot but think of him among still heavier losses: he was my earliest friend, and would have taught me wisdom."

ESSEX.

" Pastoral poetry, my dear Spenser, doth not require tears and lamentations. Dry thine eyes; rebuild thine house: the queen and council, I venture to promise thee, will make ample amends for every evil thou hast sustained. What! does that enforce thee to wail still louder?"

SPENSER.

" Pardon me, bear with me, most noble heart! I have lost what no council, no queen, no Essex can restore."

ESSEX.

" We will see that! There are other

swords, and other arms to wield them, besides a Leicester's and a Raleigh's. Others can crush their enemies and serve their friends."

SPENSER.

" O my sweet child ! And of many so powerful, many so wise and so beneficent, was there none to save thee ? None! none!"

ESSEX.

" I now perceive that thou lamentest what almost every father is destined to lament. Happiness must be bought, although the payment may be delayed. Consider ; the same calamity might have befallen thee here in London. Neither the houses of ambassadors, nor the palaces of kings, nor the altars of God himself, are asylums against death. How do I know but under this very roof there may sleep some latent calamity, that in an instant shall cover with gloom every inmate of the house, and every far dependant ?"

SPENSER.

" God avert it !"

ESSEX.

" Every day, every hour of the year, do hundreds mourn what thou mournest."

SPENSER.

" Oh, no, no, no! Calamities there are around us; calamities there are all over the earth; calamities there are in all seasons; but none in any season, none in any place, like mine."

ESSEX.

" So say all fathers, so say all husbands. Look at any old mansion-house, and let the sun shine as gloriously as it may on the golden vanes, or the arms recently quartered over the gateway, or the embayed window, and on the happy pair that haply is toying at it; nevertheless, thou mayest say that of a certainty the same fabric hath seen much sorrow within its chambers, and heard many wailings : and each time this was the heaviest stroke of all. Funerals have passed along through the stout-hearted knights upon the wainscot, and amidst the laughing nymphs upon the arras. Old servants have shaken their heads, as if somebody had deceived them, when they found that beauty and nobility could perish.

" Edmund! the things that are too true pass by us as if they were not true at all; and when they have singled us out, then only do they strike us. Thou and I must go too. Perhaps the next year may blow us away with its fallen leaves."*

SPENSER.

" For you, my lord, many years (I trust) are waiting: I never shall see those fallen leaves. No leaf, no bud will spring upon the earth before I sink into her breast for ever."

ESSEX.

" Thou, who art wiser than most men, shouldst bear with patience, equanimity, and courage, what is common to all."

* It happened so.

SPENSER.

" Enough! enough! enough! Have all men seen their infant burnt to ashes before their eyes?"

ESSEX.

" Gracious God! Merciful Father! what is this?"

SPENSER.

" Burnt alive! burnt to ashes! burnt to ashes! The flames dart their serpent tongues through the nursery-window. I cannot quit thee, my Elizabeth! I cannot lay down our Edmund. Oh these flames! they persecute, they inthrall me, they curl round my temples, they hiss upon my brain, they taunt me with their fierce, foul voices, they carp at me, they wither me, they consume me, throwing back to me a little of life, to roll and suffer in, with their fangs upon me. Ask me, my lord, the things you wish to know from me — I may answer them — I am now composed again. Command me, my gracious lord! I would yet serve you — soon I shall be unable. You have stooped to raise me up; you have borne with me; you have pitied me, even like one not powerful; you have brought comfort, and will leave it with me; for gratitude is comfort.

" Oh! my memory stands all a tip-toe on one burning point: when it drops from it, then it perishes. Spare me: ask me nothing; let me weep before you in peace — the kindest act of greatness."

ESSEX.

" I should rather have dared to mount into the midst of the conflagration than I now dare entreat thee not to weep. The tears that overflow thy heart, my Spenser, will staunch and heal it in their sacred stream, but not without hope in God."

SPENSER.

" My hope in God is that I may soon see again what he has taken from me. Amidst the myriads of angels there is not one so beautiful: and even he, if there be any, who is appointed my guardian, could never love me so. Ah! these are idle thoughts, vain wanderings, distempered dreams. If there ever were guardian angels, he who so wanted one, my helpless boy, would not have left these arms upon my knees."

ESSEX.

" God help and sustain thee, too gentle Spenser! I never will desert thee. But what am I? Great they have called me! Alas, how powerless, then, and infantile is greatness in the presence of calamity!

" Come, give me thy hand: let us walk up and down the gallery. Bravely done! I will envy no more a Sidney or a Raleigh."

MEMORANDUM

BY

EPHRAIM BARNETT,

WRITTEN UPON THE INNER COVER.

STUDYING the benefit and advantage of such as by God's blessing may come after me, and willing to shew them the highways of Providence from the narrow by-lane in the which it hath been his pleasure to station me, and being now advanced full-nigh unto the close and consummation of my earthly pilgrimage, methinks I cannot do better, at this juncture, than preserve the looser and lesser records of those who have gone before me in the same, with higher heel-piece to their shoe and more polished scallop to their beaver. And here, beforehand, let us think gravely and religiously on what the pagans, in their blindness, did call fortune, making a goddess of her, and saying,

> " One body she lifts up so high
> And suddenly, she makes him cry
> And scream as any wench might do
> That you should play the rogue unto :

> And the same Lady Light sees good
> To drop another in the mud,
> Against all hope and likelihood."*

My kinsman, Jacob Eldridge, having been taught by me, among other useful things, to write a fair and laudable hand, was recommended and introduced by our worthy townsman, Master Thomas Greene, unto the Earl of Essex, to keep his accounts, and to write down sundry matters from his dictation, even letters occasionally. For although our nobility, very unlike the French, not only can read and write, but often do, yet some from generosity, and some from dignity, keep in their employment what those who are illiterate, and would not appear so, call an *amanuensis*, thereby meaning *secretary* or *scribe*. Now it happened that our gracious queen's highness was desirous

---

* The editor has been unable to discover who was the author of this very free translation of an Ode in Horace. He is certainly happy in his amplification of the *stridore acuto*. May it not be surmised that he was some favourite scholar of Ephraim Barnett?

of knowing all that could be known about the Rebellion in Ireland; and hearing but little truth from her nobility in that country, even the fathers in God inclining more unto court favour than will be readily believed of spiritual lords, and moulding their ductile depositions on the pasteboard of their temporal mistress, until she was angry at seeing the lawn-sleeves so besmerched from wrist to elbow, she herself did say unto the Earl of Essex,—

" Essex! these fellows lie! I am inclined to unfrock and scourge them sorely for their leasings. Of that anon. Find out, if you can, somebody who hath his wit and his honesty about him at the same time. I know that when one of these paniers is full the other is apt to be empty, and that men walk crookedly for want of balance. No matter — we must search and find. Persuade — thou canst persuade, Essex!—say any thing, do any thing. We must talk gold and give—iron. Dost understand me?"

The earl did kiss the jewels upon the dread fingers, for only the last joint of each is visible : and surely no mortal was ever so fool-hardy as to take such a monstrous liberty as touching it, except in spirit! On the next day there did arrive many fugitives from Ireland ; and among the rest was Master Edmund Spenser, known even in those parts for his rich vein of poetry, in which he is declared by our best judges to excel the noblest of the ancients, and to leave all the moderns at his feet. Whether he notified his arrival unto the earl, or whether fame brought the notice thereof unto his lordship, Jacob knoweth not. But early in the morrow did the earl send for Jacob, and say unto him,

" Eldridge! thou must write fairly and clearly out, and in somewhat large letters, and in lines somewhat wide apart, all that thou hearest of the conversation I shall hold with a gentleman from Ireland. Take this gilt and illumined vellum, and albeit the civet make thee sick fifty times, write upon it all that passes! Come not out of the closet until the gentleman hath gone homeward. The queen requireth much exactness; and this is equally a man of genius, a man of business, and a man of worth. I expect from him not only what is true, but what is the most important and necessary to understand rightly and completely; and nobody in existence is more capable of giving me both information and advice. Perhaps if he thought another were within hearing he would be offended or over-cautious. His delicacy and mine are warranted safe and sound by the observance of those commands which I am delivering unto thee."

It happened, as will be seen, that no information was given in this conference relating to the movements or designs of the rebels. So that Master Jacob Eldridge was left possessor of the costly vellum, which, now Master Spenser is departed this life, I keep as a memorial of him, albeit oftener than once I have taken.

pounce-box and pen-knife in hand, in order to make it a fit and proper vehicle for my own very best writing. But I pretermitted it, finding that my hand is no longer the hand it was, or rather that the breed of geese is very much degenerated, and that their quills, like men's manners, are grown softer and flaccider. Where it will end God only knows; I shall not live to see it.

Alas, poor Jacob Eldridge! he little thought that within twelve months his glorious master, and the scarcely less glorious poet, would be no more! In the third week of the following year was Master Edmund buried at the charges of the earl; and within these few days hath this lofty nobleman bowed his head under the axe of God's displeasure; such being our gracious queen's. My kinsman Jacob sent unto me by the Alcester drover, old Clem Fisher, this, among other papers, fearing the wrath of that offended highness, which allowed not her own sweet disposition to question or thwart the will divine. Jacob did likewise tell me in his letter, that he was sure I should be happy to hear the success of William Shakspeare, our townsman. And in truth right glad was I to hear of it, being a principal in bringing it about, as those several sheets will shew which have the broken tile laid upon them to keep them down compactly.

Jacob's words are these :—

" Now I speak of poets, you will be in a maze at hearing that our townsman hath written a power of matter for the playhouse. Neither he nor the booksellers think it quite good enough to print: but I do assure you, on the faith of a Christian, it is not bad; and there is rare fun in the last thing of his about Venus, where a Jew, one Shiloh, is choused out of his money and his revenge. However, the best critics and the greatest lords find fault, and very justly, in the words,

' Hath not a Jew eyes? hath not a Jew hands, organs, dimensions, senses, affections, passions? fed with the same food, hurt with the same weapons, subject to the same diseases, healed by the same means, warmed and cooled by the same winter and summer, as a Christian is?'

"Surely this is very unchristianlike. Nay, for supposition sake, suppose it to be true, was it his business to tell the people so? Was it his duty to ring the crier's bell and cry to them, *the sorry Jews are quite as much men as you are?* The impudentest thing (excepting some bauderies) that ever came from the stage! The church, luckily, has let him alone for the present; and the queen winks upon it. The best defence he can make for himself is, that it comes from the mouth of a Jew, who says many other things as abominable. Master Greene may over-rate him; but Master Greene declares that if William goes on improving and taking his advice, it will be desperate hard work in another seven years to find so many as half-a-dozen chaps equal to him within the liberties. Master Greene and myself took him with us to see the burial of Master Edmund Spenser in Westminster Abbey, on the 19th of January last. The halberdmen pushed us back as having no business there. Master Greene told them he belonged to the queen's company of players. William Shakspeare could have said the same, but did not. And I, fearing that Master Greene and he might be halberded back into the crowd, shewed the badge of the Earl of Essex. Whereupon did the serjeant ground his halberd, and say unto me,—

" ' That badge commands admittance every where : your folk likewise may come in.'

" Master Greene was red-hot angry, and told me he would bring him before the *council*.

" William smiled, and Master Greene said,

" ' Why ! would not you, if you were in my place ?'

" He replied,

" ' I am an half inclined to do worse — to bring him before the *audience* some spare hour.'

" At the close of the burial-service all the poets of the age threw their pens into the grave, together with the pieces they had composed in praise or lamentation of the deceased. William Shakspeare was the only poet who abstained from throwing in either pen or poem,— at which no one marvelled, he being of low estate, and the others not having yet taken him by the hand. Yet many authors recognised him, not indeed as author, but as player; and one, civiller than the rest, came up unto him triumphantly, his eyes sparkling with glee and satisfaction, and said consolatorily,

" ' In due time, my honest friend, you may be admitted to do as much for one of us.'

" ' After such encouragement," replied our townsman, " I am bound in duty to give you the preference, should I indeed be worthy.'

" This was the only smart thing he uttered all the remainder of the day; during the whole of it he appeared to be half lost, I know not whether in melancholy or in meditation, and soon left us."

Here endeth all that my kinsman Jacob

wrote about William Shakspeare, saving and excepting his excuse for having written so much. The rest of his letter was on a matter of wider and weightier import, namely, on the price of Cotteswolde cheese, at Evesham fair. And yet, although ingenious men be not among the necessaries of life, there is something in them that makes us curious in regard to their goings and doings. It were to be wished that some of them had attempted to be better accountants; and others do appear to have laid aside the copybook full early in the day. Nevertheless, they have their uses and their merits. Master Eldridge's letter is the wrapper of much wholesome food for contemplation. Although the decease (within so brief a period) of such a poet as Master Spenser, and such a patron as the earl, be unto us appalling, we laud and magnify the great Disposer of events, no less for his goodness in raising the humble than for his power in extinguishing the great. And peradventure ye, my heirs and descendants, who shall read with due attention what my pen now writeth, will say with the royal Psalmist, that it inditeth of a good matter, when it sheweth unto you that, whereas it pleased the queen's highness to send a great lord before the judgment-seat of Heaven, háving fitted him by means of such earthly instruments as princes in like cases do usually employ, and deeming (no doubt) in her princely heart, that by such shrewd tonsure his head would be best fitted for a crown of glory, and thus doing all that she did out of the purest and most considerate love for him. It likewise hath pleased her highness to use her right-hand as freely as her left, and to raise up a second burgess of our town to be one of her company of players. And ye, also, by industry and loyalty, may cheerfully hope for promotion in your callings, and come up (some of you) as nearly to him in the presence of royalty, as he cometh up (far off indeed at present) to the great and wonderful poet, who lies dead among more spices than any

phœnix, and more quills than any porcupine.
If this thought may not prick and incitate you,
little is to be hoped from any gentle admonition, or any earnest expostulation, of

Your loving friend and kinsman,

E. B.

ANNO ÆT. SUÆ 74, DOM. 1599,

DECEMB. 16;

GLORIA DP. DF. ET DSS.

AMOR VERSUS VIRGINEM REGINAM!

PROTESTANTICE LOQUOR ET HONESTO SENSU:

OBTESTOR CONSCIENTIAM MEAM!

THE END.

LONDON:
J. MOYES, CASTLE STREET, LEICESTER SQUARE.

VII.

In 3 vols, post 8vo.

JACOB FAITHFUL.

By the Author of " PETER SIMPLE."

" It is full of incident, and will, we doubt not, be a universal favourite."—
Literary Gazette.

VIII.

Third Edition.   Price 16*s.* bound.

MR. LODGE'S PEERAGE FOR 1834.

" A work which corrects all the errors of former works.   It is the production
of a herald, we had almost said by birth, but certainly by profession and studies
—Mr. Lodge, the Norroy King of Arms."—*Times.*

IX.

In 2 vols. post 8vo.

THE INFIRMITIES OF GENIUS.

By Dr. MADDEN, Author of " TRAVELS IN TURKEY."

" A very valuable and interesting work, full of new views and curious deduc-
tions."—*Literary Gazette.*

X.

Third Edition Revised.   In 3 vols. post 8vo.

PETER SIMPLE.

By the Author of " THE NAVAL OFFICER," " THE
KING'S OWN," &c.

" This is the best work Captain Marryatt has yet produced."—*Atlas.*
" ' Peter Simple' is certainly the most amusing of Captain Marryatt's amusing
novels ; a species of picture quite unique ; a class by themselves, full of humour,
truth, and graphic sketches."—*Literary Gazette.*
" This is an admirable work, and worthy of the noble service it is written to
illustrate."—*Spectator.*

XI.

In 3 vols. post 8vo.   New Edition, with a New Preface.

THE WONDROUS TALE OF ALROY.

By the Author of " VIVIAN GREY."

" Massive grandeur, luxuriant magnificence, and fancy absolutely prodigal
of its wealth, are the most characteristic features in this extraordinary emana-
tion of creative genius."—*Foreign Quarterly.*

XII.

New and Revised Edition, in 3 vols. post 8vo.

THE HAMILTONS.

By the Author of " MOTHERS AND DAUGHTERS."

" This is a fashionable novel, and one of the highest grade."—*Athenæum.*
" Mrs. Gore is undeniably one of the wittiest writers of the present day.
' The Hamiltons' is a most lively, clever, and entertaining work." — *Literary
Gazette.*
" The design of the book is new, and the execution excellent."—*Examiner.*